Going for Great

Carolee
Brockmann

American Girl

Published by Pleasant Company Publications
©1999 by Carolee Brockmann

Visit our Web site at **www.americangirl.com**

Printed in the United States of America.
First Edition
99 00 01 02 03 04 05 RRD 10 9 8 7 6 5 4 3 2 1

The characters and events portrayed in this book are fictitious.
Any similarity to real persons, living or dead, is coincidental
and not intended by the author.

American Girl™ and AG Fiction™ are trademarks of Pleasant Company.

Editorial Development: Andrea Weiss, Michelle Watkins
Art Direction and Design: Kym Abrams
Production: Kendra Pulvermacher, Pat Tuchscherer
Cover Illustration: Paul Bachem

Library of Congress Cataloging-in-Publication Data
Brockmann, Carolee.
Going for great / by Carolee Brockmann.
p. cm.
Summary: Feeling abandoned by her parents and her best friend,
sixth grader Jenna worries that her severe stage fright will spoil her
performance at a flute competition—until she gets to know a class
misfit who is a good musician and an even better friend.
ISBN 1-56247-847-8   ISBN 1-56247-752-8 (pbk)
[1. Flute Fiction. 2. Stage fright Fiction.
3. Friendship Fiction.] I. Title.
PZ7.B7826Go 1999 [Fic]—dc21 99-29465 CIP

To my mother, my daughter, my sister,
Cousin Elise, and all of us girls who,
right this minute, are going for great

Going for Great

Chapter **One**

I was cleaning my flute after band practice when Heather Bardlow tugged on my sleeve.

Heather Bardlow is short and skinny, with big, blue eyes and wisps of blond hair sticking up all over. She looks like she makes her own static electricity.

"The competition—let's do it, Jenna," she said, her eyes giving off sparks.

Mr. Thompson, our band director and flute teacher, had just announced the Annual Lakeville College Competition for Instrumental Soloists. It's a pretty big deal. And for the first time ever, it was being opened up to sixth graders. Probably because it was being held at our school this year. Franklin

Middle School has this brand-new auditorium that everyone wants to use.

Mr. Thompson had looked me straight in the eye when he made the announcement, but I looked away. I can play pretty well for a sixth grader, but a competition? A solo? I haven't performed by myself since—geez, since the third-grade talent show when I experienced my first case of stage fright. My stomach had suddenly started thumping like it was trying to trade places with my heart. Now, even the thought of a recital makes me worry about losing lunch.

Heather didn't seem to notice that I was shaking my head.

"Let's go for it, Jenna," she said. Kids called her Heather Featherbrain because, well, she looks like she's coming and going at the same time. She wears these funny old plaid skirts with T-shirts and knee socks. Today one knee sock was black and the other was dark blue. The blue one was falling down.

"*Let's?* It's not a duet, Heather."

"I know, but we could practice together—you know, coach each other and stuff."

Right. She could coach me out of stage fright and I could coach her on sock matching. I shook my head and snapped my flute case shut.

Heather moved closer. Now her eyes were soft.

"You know you could do it, Jen. You're good. You just need to stick with it."

My ears tingled. Was it that obvious that I'd skipped practicing last night and spent the time talking on the phone with Caitlin instead? I thought I had slid by OK in practice today, but maybe not.

Someone at the music room door snickered. It was Michelle Rafferty. "Oops, a private moment," she said sarcastically.

Heather looked up. Michelle cast a downward glance at Heather's socks. She cocked her head so a brown curl fell on her cheek. Michelle was the new girl in our sixth-grade class. She must have come from a town where people get what they want by flinging their hair around. It drove me nuts. She was trying to make me feel dumb for talking to Heather. That drove me nuts, too. In our town, you can talk to anyone you want to talk to.

Michelle touched her curl. "Caitlin never said you had a special musical friend, Jenna."

Special musical friend? She said it like it was some dread disease. Heather was weird, but she was an unbelievable flute player. And why would Michelle care what Caitlin said or didn't say about me? Caitlin was *my* best friend. Ever since kindergarten. Long before Michelle got here.

I wanted to say something clever or witty or mean to Michelle, but I couldn't think of anything. Heather was tracing a circle on the blue speckled carpeting with her scuffed sneaker.

I cleared my throat importantly. "Heather and I were just discussing a competition we're entering. It's only for the very best musicians in the school." I tried to sound like one of the very best musicians in the school. "And now, if you'll excuse us, we're late for French."

Michelle stepped back into the hallway. She looked impressed. Heather slipped me a smile. I realized what I had said and almost fainted.

Chapter **Two**

I got through French class and the rest of the day by refusing to think one single thought about the competition. But the thought kept creeping back. And I had to admit it. Part of me wanted to be in that competition. I wanted to go for it.

My flute banged against my knee as Caitlin and I walked home from school. Through its case, I could feel it begging me for a chance.

Caitlin Oliveira and I have walked home from school together just about every day since kindergarten. I live two blocks from school, and Caitlin lives around the corner from me. She's a little taller than I am, and thinner. She looks like a ballerina. We both have dark hair. Cat's is long and thick, and she wears it down her back in one braid. I got mine cut short last year, just past my ears. On good days it curves up toward my chin. Today was a good hair day, but so far not as good for my stomach. And Caitlin was being no help.

"Jenna Dowling, star flutist of Franklin Middle School!" she announced, lettering a banner in the air with her fingers.

I sighed. "Yeah, right. First just get me past the preliminaries."

Each school in the county would hold its own preliminary qualifier the first week of May. The students who qualified would move on to the one, the only, Lakeville College Competition for Instrumental Soloists, on May 14th. The entry form felt like lead in my backpack.

Caitlin was bubbling away. "There you'll be, the star of Franklin Middle School, stepping out onto that stage and standing there, all alone, in the spotlight. Just you and your flute . . ."

I gulped.

"Then, you'll start to play." She brought an imaginary flute up to her mouth. "Everyone will listen. Seventh graders, eighth graders, high schoolers—even college kids!"

Caitlin stopped and looked at me with big eyes. "Jenna, college kids'll hear you play."

My stomach heaved.

"Geez, Jen, *I've* never even heard you play before. Hey, how come?"

My stomach would have answered if I'd let it, but I just shrugged, nonchalantly. "Don't know."

I knew. I hated anything that meant having to stand up in front of people. Book reports gave me toxic shock, and even reciting a sentence in French class made my bones quiver. The concert band I could deal with—safety in numbers. But what was I doing thinking about a solo? I shuddered. Caitlin would never understand.

Caitlin looked thoughtfully at me. "So, are you any good?"

Mr. Thompson thought I was. And my mom always said she liked listening when I practiced.

"Yeah, I think so."

"Well, then, how come this competition thing's making you so green?" Caitlin asked.

My stomach was rising like high tide. Huge purple fear monsters started crashing like waves against the inside of my head. If I even uttered the words *stage fright,* I was sure a tidal wave of fear would drown me. Then I'd never be able to walk onto the stage. Caitlin was my best friend. I wanted to tell her about my problem, but I just couldn't. I took a deep breath and mentally shoved the sea monsters back underwater.

"Just a little nervous, is all," I said.

Caitlin started walking again. "Hey! Do you remember how jumpy we got before that gymnastics demonstration?"

Gymnastics. I laughed. My stomach settled. Gymnastics was different. It was just for fun. Besides, I wasn't really any good. Caitlin was. She could do round-offs and back handsprings, and she was even learning a routine on the uneven parallel bars. I was just thrilled with a decent cartwheel.

"Don't you ever get scared, Cat?" I asked.

"Of what? Falling?"

"No, just being out there in front of everyone."

She shook her head. "Not really. I stop, take a deep breath, and—" Caitlin threw down her books and flipped onto my front yard. She landed perfectly, missing the March mud of our tulip bed by inches. No purple monsters in that head. Cat loves drama. She loves adventure. She really loves it when everyone's looking at her.

Caitlin stretched her long body into that sleek arched pose that all the Olympic gymnasts finish their routines with. My mom was at the front door waiting for us. She started applauding.

Mom was still in her work clothes. And today she had on serious work clothes. She usually wears the black suit and the red silk blouse for really important meetings. It looks great with her dark hair and fair complexion. She's tall and thin, and I think she should be a model, but she says she's more the business type. She works part-time at an advertising agency.

I ran to the door and grabbed an imaginary microphone. "Now that you've won the gold, Caitlin Oliveira, what are you going to do next?"

This was our standard Olympics joke. It was perfect for almost any occasion: "Now that you've passed your spelling test, Jenna Dowling . . ." or "Now that you've finished that entire double-chocolate fudge sundae, Caitlin Oliveira . . ." or "Now that you've turned eleven . . ."

Caitlin and I chanted the answer together. "Buy Crunchy-Crispos, of course!"

Mom's ad agency has been trying to get the Crunchy-Crispos cereal account for what seems like a zillion years. She's always trying to think of clever slogans and jingles for it. Caitlin and I made up this one: "Crunchy-Crispos are a treat. They make us crunch from head to feet. When we eat them we feel complete!"

"OK, you advertising geniuses, break it up,"

said Mom. "I've got to get Jenna to her place of employment." On Fridays Mom drives me over to the Petersons' house to babysit their three-year-old daughter, Meggie.

Mrs. Peterson is the hostess at the Café Venezia on Fridays. I stay with Meggie till Mr. Peterson gets home from work. It's only an hour and a half or so, but Meggie's a handful—actually, she's supercharged. Mom says "busier than a bee." I say "toddler tyranny."

I jumped into the car and rolled down the window. "What's up for this weekend, Caitlin?"

"Gram's house!" she shouted, gathering her books and thrusting her fist into the air. "Yes!"

Her grandmother's house is really an inn out in the country. It's a huge old Victorian house. Every room has a canopy bed, lacy pillows, and different patterns of tiny delicate flower prints on the wallpaper. Out in the back there's an apple orchard and a stable with four horses. I've never stayed at the inn overnight, but once I went with Caitlin for the day. We had tea in a real parlor, and then Alfie, the stable hand, took us out for a ride in a horse and buggy. I smelled apple blossoms and felt like I was a character in one of those Laura Ingalls Wilder books.

"Lucky!" I shouted back to her.

"Gram said we could all come for a weekend this spring—you, me, maybe Michelle. We just have to wait for a weekend that's not filled up with guests."

Mom started the car. I waved good-bye to Caitlin. "See ya!"

Maybe *Michelle*? Why did Caitlin want to invite Michelle? I thought of the bouncing brown curls and frowned. She didn't belong at the inn—the way she snickered at Heather and me today in the music room. Then the competition came back to me in a rush. My stomach lurched.

"You got quiet all of a sudden," Mom said as we pulled up in front of the Peterson house.

I opened the car door. Now was not the time for confessions about purple fear monsters, tidal waves, and a musical competition. I looked at my watch. Mrs. Peterson and a monster of the three-year-old kind were waiting for me. I forced a smile and pointed at Mom's black skirt.

"Hey, you're wearing the power suit."

"You know it, Jen-girl," sighed Mom. "Power— that's the word of the hour." Sometimes she can't help talking in rhyme.

"Big doings at work?" I asked.

"Big doings. I'll tell you all about it at dinner."

Chapter **Three**

Meggie was only in low gear today. We sat and colored. Then we sat and played with her dollhouse. All that sitting gave me too much time for thinking.

I tried pushing the competition out of my mind. I kept telling myself, *Later. Worry later. It's only March. The competition isn't until May.* I decided that when I got home I'd relax and have dinner with Mom. Then I'd do my homework and fill out the entry form. Entry form! My heart stumbled at the thought. I took a deep breath and tried to be stern with myself. *It's only a piece of paper. All you have to do is write your name, address, and age.* NO BIG DEAL.

Meggie handed me the Mommy doll. Absent-mindedly, I sat her on the dollhouse roof. "Help, Meggie, help!" I yelled in a Mommy-doll voice. "Get me down from here!"

Meggie giggled. She scrambled across the room and came back with her big red hook-and-ladder truck.

She cupped her pudgy little hands around her mouth and boomed, "Emergency! Emergency!"

It was an emergency all right. What I really needed was a big red fire truck to save me from myself. Why did I have to open my big mouth in front of Michelle? Who did I think I was, entering some competition for college kids? Things were going fine just the way they were. Why did Heather go and get me all worked up about playing the stupid flute?

Meggie and I spent the rest of the afternoon saving the Mommy doll from the back of the sofa, the kitchen counter, and other high places. Meggie loved it when I put the plastic Mommy in the mixing bowl and yelled, "Help me! Help me! I'm all mixed up!"

When Mr. Peterson finally dropped me off at home, I could detect the delicious dinner smells all the way out in the driveway. I started to feel better. There's nothing like a good dose of Mom's cooking to cure just about anything. I opened the door, and the aroma of lasagna wrapped itself around me.

"Hey, Mom! Lasagna!"

She was in the kitchen. Another smell hit me.

"Wow! Fresh-baked bread, too!" Every once in a while my mom goes crazy and makes her own bread. She says the kneading is therapeutic. But she also knows it's my all-time favorite. She must have made the dough this morning. Something was definitely up.

"It's not my birthday, ya know."

She smiled and brushed a strand of black hair out of her eyes. They had that "Are you ready for this?" look.

Uh-oh. Why did I suddenly feel like my stomach was in for another ride? It couldn't be bad news. Mom looked too happy. I went to the sink to wash my hands. A million thoughts flowed over me as the water splashed through my fingers. *She won the Crunchy-Crispos account. That would explain the power suit. Or maybe she's getting transferred and we're moving. No. Bigger. They're having a baby! No, wait. Dad got a raise. Dad's coming home early. That's it! Dad finally got a desk job.* I knew they'd been talking about it. He said he would be up for a promotion soon. That would make Mom ecstatic.

My dad's a merchant marine. He works on a ship out at sea. That means when he's working, he's gone. He usually works three or four months and then takes a month off. Four months away is a long time. But he's had this job ever since I was born. When I was little I used to get scared because I'd forget what he looked like. Then Mom gave me a laminated picture of me and Dad. I would chew on it when I missed him.

The good part is that when Dad comes home, he's home. And he loves our house. One morning I came downstairs and I thought I saw him hugging the kitchen wall. I wasn't that surprised. He had his cheek against it and one eye was closed. Then I saw the spatula in his hand and a can of putty at his feet. He was patching a tiny crack in the plaster, really carefully. He loves to patch and mend and shine up the little things that most people wouldn't even notice.

I don't chew on his picture anymore, but some-times when Mom's not around I try to find that patched place in the kitchen and put my cheek against the wall. I can almost feel Dad's heartbeat in the house.

I dried my hands and grinned. When Dad called later I would tell him about the competition and even about the stage fright. He'd know what to do.

We talk to him every Friday night. Last Friday he called from off the shore of Puerto Rico. He's been to Japan, the Antarctic—all over the world. He brings back awesome presents. I have a jar of black sand from Hawaii and a tiny rice bowl, with a bull's-eye painted on the bottom, from Hong Kong. The presents are great, but having Dad around all the time would be a million times better.

Mom wouldn't say a word until we sat down at the table. The lasagna was perfect—crispy on the top and stringy with cheese, but I was almost too excited to taste it.

Mom took a deep breath, and the extra oxygen seemed to light a fire in her eyes. "I got a promotion, Jenna."

I jumped up to hug her. "That's great, Mom."

But I was confused. What about Dad's desk job? What about Dad coming home?

She took my hands in hers. "It's what I've been working for. I'll have my own staff and all my own accounts, Jen.

I smiled. "Crunchy-Crispos?"

She nodded. "I'll get that one by hook or by crook! But it means I'll be working full-time."

I felt my smile tugging down. "Every day?"

"Every day from nine to five."

"Oh," I said. I wanted to say, "Hey, great. If I

can babysit Meggie Peterson, I can certainly babysit myself." But all I could think of was how empty the house would be every day at three o'clock. I burst into tears.

Mom pulled me onto her lap, and I sat there sobbing like a baby. She must have read my mind. "Shhhh. It won't be so bad. Mrs. Oliveira will drive you to gymnastics on Tuesdays and Thursdays, and then you can go home with Caitlin. And now that it's getting nicer out, I thought you could ride your bike to the Petersons on Fridays."

I snuffled. "Does Dad know?"

"I talked to him on Wednesday."

So Dad knew on Wednesday, and by Friday Mom already had my life rearranged. She made it seem like no big deal, just a matter of carpooling and nice weather. Even Caitlin's mom knew about this before I did. Did anyone ever consider discussing it with me?

I wanted to call Caitlin and tell her I was now officially a latchkey kid, but she was on her way to her Gram's inn by now. And anyway, we were waiting for Dad to call.

I was lying on my bed pretending to do my homework when the phone finally rang. I heard Mom talking in a low voice and then her extra-cheerful "Jen-girl, it's your dad."

I rolled off my bed and reached across the floor for the phone. I have this black-and-white-checkered bathroom rug—the fuzzy kind—that I lie on when I talk to Caitlin. But now I picked the whole phone up and crawled back onto my bed. "Good news about Mom's promotion, huh?"

He started to answer with some pep-talk stuff about independence and growing up, but I interrupted him. "And you know, it works out OK, because I'm entering this musical competition, so I have to spend lots of time practicing."

"Oh!" He sounded surprised. "Will I be home for this event?" he asked.

I sighed. "No. It's May 14th. And it's not open to the public."

"I'm not the public! I'm your dad."

"This isn't a school assembly, Dad. It's a competition. With real judges."

"And they don't want pushy parents getting in the way?"

"Yeah, probably."

"Is there a prize?"

I wasn't sure. What was I expecting? Money? Fame? Total embarrassment? "I don't know. I don't really care, I guess—just as long as I do my best," I said.

"Hello? Hello, ship to shore?" said Dad. "Is this Jenna *Dowling*?"

"Da-ad!"

"Sorry, sweetie, that just sounded altogether too mature."

"Daddy?"

"What?"

I wanted to ask him what I should do about the fear monsters, but I realized I had already told him what I was going to do. "Nothing."

"OK, Jenna Dowling. With me or without me, I know you'll be the greatest."

"Well, I don't know about the greatest . . ."

"Why not, Jenna? You have to go for it! Don't just settle for good enough. Go for *great*."

I nodded and thought of Heather's sparking eyes.

Dad was coming home June 1st. But I always asked him the same question at the end of our phone calls. And he always answered the same way. It was a ritual we started when I was little.

"When are you coming home, Daddy?"

"Not soon enough, sweetie."

Chapter **Four**

Over the weekend I didn't pick up my flute once. I didn't fill out the stupid competition form, and I didn't tell Mom about it. On Monday I avoided Heather Bardlow all day long.

It was Mom's first day working full-time. I showed Caitlin my house key as we walked home from school.

"Whoa," she said. It was on a silver chain around my neck. Caitlin poked at it like it was forbidden treasure. A necklace. Big deal. Mom was obviously feeling guilty about replacing herself with a key.

"Just think—the whole house to yourself!"

"So?"

"So, I don't know. Parties, loud music, Roller-blading in the kitchen?"

I came home and let myself in. I looked at the spotless kitchen floor. Yeah, right, I thought. I don't even own Rollerblades. I ate a jumbo-size bag of potato chips and watched an old movie. At 5:25 I threw some hot dogs in a pot of water and opened a can of beans. I picked up a loaf of bread, left over from our lasagna dinner, and slammed it down onto the cutting board. I sawed off a couple of stale hunks.

Mom burst in the door. "What's this I smell? Dinner?"

I grunted.

She took off her coat and put down her brief-case. "Looks like you've lost a chauffeur and I've gained a chef."

"Hot dogs hardly count as cooking."

"I know, honey. But I appreciate it." She looked at her watch. "Five forty-two. Not too bad. We still have the whole evening. Come on, let's eat and I'll tell you all about my new plan for winning the Crunchy-Crispos account, and you can tell me what's news with youse."

I couldn't stay mad at Mom. I looked at her. Her eyes were sparkling. I thought of Dad's words, "Don't just settle for good enough. Go for great."

Mom was going for great with Crunchy-Crispos and her advertising stuff.

But I wasn't ready to tell her about my own competition yet. I needed to get into the swing of this home-alone thing first. One major life change at a time.

When Heather Bardlow plays the flute, her neck rises up like a swan lifting into the sky, and she closes her eyes. Her flute is old and kind of scuffed up, and there's a dent on one end, but her notes come out pure and whole. She was playing the eighth-note exercise at our Tuesday advanced group. When Heather plays, everyone listens. Even if it's just an exercise. And she was making this one sound like a bubbling stream, the kind you want to sit next to on a big, mossy rock. I was watching her fingers move and thinking about strands of sunlight filtering down through the trees.

I closed my eyes. This was a place I could take Mom and Dad to. Maybe on a picnic. It would be in the middle of the week. Mom would pull me out of bed that morning and say, "This is a day for neither school nor work!" She'd call in sick and leave her Crunchy-Crispos folder at home. We'd pack a lunch and sit by the stream and talk and laugh. I'd

play my flute for my parents, and they'd congratu-
late me for doing so well at the competition . . .

Somebody giggled, and I thought I heard Mr.
Thompson call my name. I put my flute to my lips
and started to play.

"Jenna, I just asked if anybody had any entry
forms for me. They're due tomorrow. And I have
the music here for the competition."

My face got hot. Why was I constantly on the
verge of tears lately?

"Sorry, Mr. Thompson."

"No need to apologize." He turned to the rest of
the flute class and stroked his short silvery beard.
"Always take every opportunity to get lost in music."

After the lesson Heather and I stayed to clean
our flutes like we always do. "You really sounded
good today," I said.

She was wearing a gold T-shirt with *Mike's Bar
and Grill* printed across the front, with her usual
red plaid skirt. Both knee socks were white. Not
both the same size—one hit her knee and the other
stopped about midcalf—but they were both very
white. She looked up from under her blond frizzles
of hair and smiled.

"Want me to help you fill out those forms?"
she asked.

"No, I don't need any help. I just haven't had a

chance yet." Well, that wasn't exactly true. I just hadn't wanted to yet.

"We could sit in the back during French and do it. It's really easy. And as soon as you hand in the form, you get the sheet music." She showed me the three pieces of music she'd just gotten from Mr. Thompson. There was a *menuett* by Friedrich Kuhlau and a *bourrée* by Handel. The third piece was a Beethoven minuet.

Beethoven! This was really the big time. Serious music for serious musicians.

I usually sat with Caitlin in French, but she would have to understand. I couldn't wait to get my hands on the music.

"*Comment allez-vous?*"

We slipped in the door just as Ms. Buttner was starting the class. She always says, "Co-mon-tally voo?" which means "How are you?" in French. We're supposed to answer, "Tray byen, ay voo?" which means "Very well, and you?"

Everybody loves French class because it's a chance to go to a different room with a different teacher. And it's easy, kind of like kindergarten again. We're learning colors, numbers, and letters. *Ecoutez et répétez.* I love how Ms. Buttner says that:

"Ay-coo-tay ay ray-pay-tay." It means "listen and repeat." And it's fun—as long as I don't have to get up and *répétez* all by myself.

I waved to Caitlin, who was sitting up front with Sherri Rosa, and plunked into a seat in back. Heather slid in next to me.

Ms. Buttner started us off on the alphabet, and I pulled out the competition form.

"Musical experience?" I whispered to Heather.

"Just write down how long you've been taking flute," Heather whispered back, pretending she was scratching her nose so Ms. Buttner wouldn't see her lips moving.

"Osh, ee, zhee, kah, el, em . . ." Ms. Buttner always did a little dance with the alphabet to keep the class together. She wasn't paying any attention to us in the back.

"Since third grade," I wrote. Then I filled in my name, address, and age.

"Third grade? Me too! Want to come over after school to rehearse?"

"I can't. I've got gymnastics."

Heather frowned and tapped her chin. "What about tomorrow?"

"OK, but you should come over to my house." I pulled the key out from under my sweater. "I've got the whole place to myself."

Ms. Buttner cleared her throat in our direction. We snapped to attention. "And now, mayz amee, because I am feeling hungry today, we will learn desserts."

Somebody cheered.

"*Ecoutez et répétez: Gateau,*" she said, holding up a picture of a cake.

Heather winked at me, and we both shouted, "GAH-TOE!" But I was thinking about Beethoven.

Chapter **Five**

"**H**ey, Mom, Jenna's doing Beethoven! The classics!" Caitlin waved the sheet music under Mrs. Oliveira's nose as we scrambled into her car after school. It was just starting to rain, and the air had that squished-worm smell of spring.

"Minuet in G," Caitlin's mom murmured, pulling her glasses down to look at the page. "Look at all those notes." She passed the music back to me.

Caitlin fastened her seat belt. "She's playing it in the Lakeville *College* competition."

I put the music back in the manila envelope. "Well, maybe. There are three pieces to practice.

Then, at the competition, right before you play, they tell you which one to do."

"What a bummer. If you were psychic you wouldn't have to waste your time practicing all three of them," Caitlin said.

"Hmmm, Minuet in G—dee-doodoodoodoo dee doot doot!" Mrs. Oliveira sang in time to the windshield wipers.

I leaned forward. "Actually, Mrs. O, that's the *Bach* Minuet in G."

Caitlin pinched my arm. "Bach? Beethoven? Jen, you're a musical genius."

I shrugged. "I listen to a lot of stuff."

"So how come I'm the last to know?"

"What are you talking about? You know you've got the best floor routine music in town thanks to me. I've got a great ear for classics to cartwheel by."

"Oh yeah. Thanks, Maestro Dowling."

We jumped out of the car, waved good-bye to Mrs. Oliveira, and ran to the big gray doors of the gymnasium.

When I came out of the locker room and into the gym, I could hear Caitlin giggling. She was bouncing on the Tumble Trak with another girl, who was nudging her and pointing at one of the instructors. I started running over to them, but my feet stalled. The other girl was Michelle Rafferty. Suddenly the gym air smelled stale and sweaty. I looked up at the high ceiling. There was a balloon from some little kid's birthday party caught in the black metal beams. It was starting to shrivel, but it couldn't float down because it was stuck in the crisscross of the beams.

I took a deep breath and plodded toward Caitlin and Michelle. When I got to the Tumble Trak, they bounced off and walked over to me. Caitlin was giggling again. Michelle nudged me with her elbow and whispered, "That one, right there, with the yellow hair. He's got it for Caitlin."

"Got what?"

"Got what?!" shrilled Michelle. She started laughing. "Got what! He *likes* her, you dopester."

Yellow hair. I looked over at Scott Anderson. He was squatting on the floor, helping a second grader do a somersault. Scott was our instructor last year. Nice, but all the instructors at gymnastics are nice. He has straight blond hair that always gets in his eyes, and huge arm muscles.

"He's *twenty*," I said.

Michelle fluffed her curls. "So? He's a babe. Maybe he'll be my spotter on the vault." She put her hands on her waist and gave a little wiggle.

"Sometimes I need just a tiny bit of help getting over that big old thing!" She grinned and poked Caitlin in the side.

I stared at Michelle. What planet was she from? But Caitlin loved it. She was already gone on another giggle trip. Some of the other girls in the class were coming over to see what was up.

"How exactly can you tell that he's 'got it' for Caitlin?" I asked.

"I don't know." Michelle smiled at me slyly. "I can just tell."

I bit my lip, trying not to laugh. We all looked over at Scott. Apparently his deep love for Caitlin was inspiring him to send a troop of second graders through a somersault routine. I suddenly had the image of Cat bringing Scott to a sixth-grade dance. They would both be dressed in Lycra and wearing headbands with those big intertwined Olympic O's. I started giggling.

Luckily, Ann the Amazon interrupted us. That's what we call our instructor. She's about six feet tall and has red hair that she pulls back into a ponytail. She came loping up to the Tumble Trak and blew her whistle.

"I'm late. You're laughing." She clapped her long hands. "You stars warmed up yet? No, huh? Well, laps—all of you!"

As we started running, she pointed to Michelle and yelled to the group, "That's Michelle. Say hi to her. She's new."

But Michelle wasn't new at gymnastics. She was as good as Caitlin. Maybe better. And she didn't need any kind of help on the vault.

Usually Caitlin hangs back with me to give me a hand if I need it and to have a few laughs. But I was still practicing my Russian straddle on the Tumble Trak when Caitlin and Michelle finished their exercises and went across the gym to the uneven bars. Between bounces I watched them check out each other's calluses. Cat showed Michelle her new hand grips and even let her try them on. Cat did her pirouette mount and then Michelle did a mount I'd never seen before. They looked like graceful, long-winged birds. I thought of the terns that Dad pointed out to me once when I visited his ship. Michelle and Caitlin were like those sleek, slim seabirds making effortless loops over the ocean.

The Tumble Trak jiggled and jolted me each time I bounced. I wanted to soar up and join Cat and Michelle, but I didn't have any wings. I was just a bouncing, bobbing blob.

At home, I couldn't get that dead-socks gym air out of my nose. And I couldn't get that horrible bounce-bounce-bounce from the Tumble Trak out of my body. I turned on the shower and peeled off my sweaty clothes. My dad says that sometimes when you've been on a boat in heavy seas, it takes a while to get your land legs back. Even after you think you're fine, when you step into a small space the waves start rocking you again. I stepped into the shower and sure enough, the bouncing started again. I turned the dial on the nozzle to "pulsate" to try breaking the rhythm. Water pounced on my back like skipping eighth notes. Relief. The water rushed through my hair. I felt Heather's eighth notes and the Minuet in G. I didn't think about the competition, just all those soothing eighth notes raining down on me.

"Jenna? Jenna, is that you or a new CD?"

I put down my flute and looked at the clock. 6:15. Mom was late tonight.

"Who's playing such wonderful Beethoven in my house?" she called.

I grabbed my music and ran downstairs. Mom was setting the table. Her briefcase was on the kitchen counter, along with a brown bag that was giving off the unmistakable smell of meatball sandwiches. I sniffed again. Was that fresh-baked bread from the Italian bakery? I sure had to give her credit for trying.

I couldn't put off telling Mom about the competition any longer. I took another deep breath and, fortified by delicious dinner aromas, told her all about it.

"A college-level competition? That sounds pretty exciting."

That was one way to put it. "Yeah," I said, trying to squash the purple monsters before they invaded my stomach and ruined my plans for a great dinner. "I handed in the forms and got copies of the music today. That was what I was playing when you came in."

"Well, you sound terrific already, hon. Do you want a salad with your sub?"

"Sure, Mom, I'll make it." I felt bad about not getting dinner ready. I should have at least set the table. I grabbed a bowl for the lettuce. "I like the Minuet in G," I continued, "but it doesn't sound right to me as a solo. The second part, the harmony, is missing. I can't wait to try it with Heather."

"Heather?"

"She plays the flute, too. We're in it together."

"Oh." Mom ripped open the paper bag and put a sub on my plate. I carried the salad over. "Sorry, Jen, I'm thinking about three million things. You're in what together?"

"The contest."

"Right. The school flute contest."

Close enough. I took a bite of meatball. "So, what's news with youse?" I asked.

"They've pushed the Crunchy-Crispos deadline up, so everyone in the office is in a tizzy. A regular flurry of flustered fiends."

"Mom? Do you ever get really nervous about something? I mean scared?"

"Scared?"

"Like when something's really important to you, it makes your stomach jump?"

Mom glanced at her briefcase and frowned. "Deadlines can do that."

"I keep having this dream about purple sea monsters. Sometimes they're coming at me like a tidal wave . . ."

Mom smiled her you're-my-little-sweetie-pie smile. "Are you worried about Dad again? He's safe and sound, honey. I talked to him today from my office." She reached across the table and took my hand. "He'll be home soon. Try not to worry so much."

This time I wasn't worried about Dad falling overboard. I was worried about me drowning. In a sea of judges. *Try not to worry so much.* Right.

Chapter **Six**

It felt weird on Wednesday, walking home with Heather instead of Caitlin. But Caitlin had told me she had something special she had to go do after school.

I wasn't really worried about what Caitlin would think about me practicing with Heather. I had been more nervous about the idea of having Heather in my house. I couldn't picture all that static electricity in my room. But she seemed perfectly at home there. She squinted at one of my Hollywood posters and spoke through her nose, "Ah yes, how very *expressive*. It simply cries out 'we-are-at-the-mall,' does it not?"

She was funny. I tried the same snooty nasal tone. "Why yes, you're quite right," I said, waggling my fingers in the air and tilting my nose up. "I consider it . . . *très du glace.*"

"*Du glace?*" Heather snorted. "Doesn't that mean something like—"

"Ice cream!" I howled.

We collapsed on the floor and laughed till we couldn't breathe.

Heather was intense. When she laughed or even smiled, she looked just like an elf. A mischievous little sprite with pointed ears. But without warning, she could morph into a fierce-eyed pack rat. Suddenly she was at my calendar, counting out the weeks till the competition. She circled May 14th in red. The mark shot out at me like an arrow. It woke up the fear monsters, and my stomach took a purple dive.

"Here's the plan," said Heather, tapping her chin with the red pen. "We'll work together for one hour every day." She found my metal music stand, all folded up in the corner. I usually put my music on my desk to practice. "Then another hour on our own," she continued, unfolding the skinny metal legs.

I nodded and tried to breathe. The huge auditorium stage was plastered onto the front of my mind. My knees started to wobble.

"You'll have to come over to my house on the days Mom works early. I have to watch my baby sister, Suki."

Heather adjusted the music stand and put the Kuhlau *menuett* on it.

I sat down on the bed and glued my eyes to the music as Heather started to play. She worked through a page and a half and then stopped.

"I've already played through all the pieces and circled the hard parts in each one—you know, tricky fingerings and stuff. Maybe you should do that, too. Then we could conquer the circled parts and erase the circles as we learn them."

"Right." I worked to keep my voice light, in spite of the purple fear monsters that were trying to conquer me. "For the Kuhlau, I guess that means circling everything but these first two notes," I joked.

Heather looked up from her music for the first time and frowned at me. Then she laughed in a short burst. "Come on, Jenna. How about the minuet then? I heard you humming it in French class today."

I picked up the Beethoven. "Yeah, I like that one. But it's missing the harmony."

"I know. I wonder why they picked it as a solo."

"I don't know. Want to try it together?" I suggested. Together was a very calming idea.

"OK. I'll do the harmony," she offered.

The music stand was about a foot too tall for Heather. We ended up playing with her standing on a little stool behind me. We may have looked funny, but we sounded great. Better than flute class, where everyone is huffing and puffing along at different times. Heather followed my phrasing perfectly, accenting the notes just the way I did. We played as if we were breathing from the same lungs. I forgot about purple monsters, latchkeys, and Tumble Traks, and I took off like a bird with long, graceful wings.

I couldn't wait to practice with Heather again. On Thursday, I met her at her house after gymnastics. It was old and small, and the front porch was missing some boards.

"This way." Heather showed me where to step. "We're going to have to get this fixed before Suki starts walking—which will be any day now."

In the kitchen, Heather's mom was trying to feed a baby seated in a high chair. I guessed it was Suki. There were dishes and pots in the sink and piles of mail and books on the counters. There was a metal dog food bowl in one corner, with a huge, drooled-on rawhide bone next to it. When I walked across the kitchen floor, my shoes made little sticking sounds.

Heather wrinkled her nose and lifted her foot. "Apple juice. She's learning to drink from a cup."

Mrs. Bardlow stood up and put her hand out to me. "Hello, Jenna. Welcome to our mess."

"Thanks, Mrs. Bardlow." She was short like Heather, but round instead of skinny. She was wearing a white uniform and white shoes. She's a nurse at the hospital downtown. Heather told me she works nights and only gets to sleep in the daytime when the baby naps.

Heather's mom sighed. "It's time for me to get going. Suki just woke up from her nap. I changed her and gave her some applesauce. Maybe she'll play with these Cheerios while you practice."

Mrs. Bardlow gave Heather and the baby a hug. "I put in a load of towels and baby stuff. Can you throw it in the dryer when it's done?" she added.

"Sure, Mom. See you later."

Heather ran into the living room and came back with a beautiful wooden music stand. "Hurry up, Jenna. Suki's only good for about fifteen minutes with the Cheerios."

I fitted my flute together and flexed my hands. "Maybe we should start with an exercise—you know, just to warm up." I waved my fingers at

Suki. "My fingies feel kind of stiff." Suki banged her tray, and the Cheerios bounced.

Heather put her flute to her lips, but she didn't play. "Did Mr. Thompson give you those breathing exercises to practice?"

"Yeah, but I've never done them."

"You should." She pointed her flute at the music stand. "These pieces need a lot of air. The exercises are great for nerves, too."

"Nerves?"

"*Exactement.*" Heather said it with a perfect French accent—"eg-ZACT-eh-mon." It means "exactly." She used French words whenever she could. She also liked "ex" words. Sometimes she could hit both at the same time. *Exactement* was definitely one of her favorites. "You know, as in stage fright," she explained.

"Stage fright," I said and waited for my stomach to heave.

"Yeah, stage fright." Heather looked straight at me. I felt like she could see into my brain. I played a fast B-flat scale.

"You get stage fright?" I asked, trying to sound casual. I gave an inward evil eye to those purple slimes clambering into my thoughts.

"Everyone gets stage fright," she answered. "*Ex-*treme *ex-*citement. Butterflies in your stomach."

Heather was suddenly the elf again, flitting around the room, waving her flute like a wand.

I couldn't help laughing. "I see. Well, I'll keep that in mind."

"Yes. Keep that in mind." Heather was pointing her flute at me like a teacher. "And do the breathing exercises."

"*Ex*-ercises?" I started playing the eighth-note exercise at breakneck speed.

Heather jumped in and finished before me. "Beat ya!"

I never finished because I started laughing. Suki squealed with delight at our cacophony. Cacophony is the opposite of harmony. A musical mess. Suki was waving her little fists around. Suddenly she stood up in her high chair.

Heather dropped her flute and ran to catch her. Just as she was lifting Suki out, three loud bangs exploded beneath us. They sounded like gunshots. A huge black dog ran into the kitchen and started barking at the basement door. Suki's cheering turned to wailing, and the banging started again.

Heather was trying to yell something to me over the din. She wasn't smiling anymore. She had her pinched and determined rat face on.

I ran over to the high chair. "I'll take her," I shouted.

"It's the washing machine," yelled Heather. "It's unbalanced or something."

I put my arms out for Suki. That made her cry even harder, which made the dog bark louder.

"Be quiet, Seymour! Stop it!" Heather shouted at the dog. She pulled him away from the door and disappeared down the stairs. Seymour galloped after her, still barking.

Suki was shrieking. I found her playpen in the living room and put her in it.

I got down to the basement just in time to see a black rubber tube spouting soapy water like a geyser. Seymour was barking furiously. Heather was soaked. She was wrestling with the water knobs behind the washing machine, trying to shut them off. Suddenly the geyser stopped. Seymour whined and then yawned.

Heather pushed her matted hair out of her eyes. She looked exactly like a drowned rat. I started to laugh. I thought she was going to laugh too and turn back into her elf self, but she didn't. Her lips were pressed into a thin line, and her shoulders drooped.

"Why does everything have to be so hard?" she muttered.

I looked at the puddles of water on the floor. "Hey, at least I'm here to help you clean up."

Heather got the black tube connected back to the washing machine again, twisting the clamps as tightly as she could. I mopped up the floor with a bunch of rags I'd found in the corner. I stood back and held my breath as Heather started up the washing machine again. It was jerking a little, but not banging like before.

I prodded the pile of wet, dirty rags with my foot. "My mom says God gave us laundry to keep us humble. She says, 'Just when you think you're all done with it, here comes another load.' Now I guess I know what she means."

Heather nodded. "I hate doing the laundry."

"Mmmee-MAAA!" Suki was yodeling urgently above us.

I raised my eyebrows at Heather and stroked an imaginary Mr. Thompson beard. "It's never too soon to start the breathing exercises, no?"

Heather almost smiled. We ran up the stairs. I followed Heather into the living room to get Suki, then up a narrow staircase to the second floor and some even narrower stairs to her bedroom. I sat down gingerly on her bed, which was covered with a faded blue spread. Heather plopped Suki down at my feet on an orange and brown braided rug while she went into her closet to look for some dry clothes.

I looked around. Her room was a mess. It was up in the attic, so there were all these strange angles instead of a flat ceiling. And there were stacks of things everywhere. Books and books. Along one wall there was a bookshelf made out of cinder blocks and boards, but most of the books were piled on the floor. She had a junky old record player and piles of records. With the walls and ceilings angling down and the books and stuff piled up, I felt like I was in a cave with stalactites and stalagmites all around me.

Heather came out of her slanted walk-in closet wearing a huge pair of black sweats and a big purple T-shirt that said *Shackley's Hardware* on the front.

Heather noticed me reading the T-shirt. "My uncle plays softball."

"Oh, so that's what 'Mike's Bar and Grill' is."

"Yeah, he runs the league. My uncle, not Mike. I always get one of each team's shirts. Brrr, I'm cold." She reached under her bed and pulled out a red Mickey Mouse sweatshirt and a couple of dust balls. She flicked the dust onto the floor. I muffled a sneeze. The red sweatshirt was too small for her. It made the purple T-shirt stick out like a tutu over the bulge of the black sweats. Heather was obviously not a girl who spent a lot of time worrying about her wardrobe. This outfit made her plaid skirt and knee socks seem absolutely fashionable. I prayed she wouldn't show up in school like this tomorrow. Michelle would have a field day.

I opened my mouth to say—exactly what, I wasn't sure. But Heather was already scooping Suki up and heading back downstairs. I watched their two heads bobbing out of the little room, and it occurred to me that maybe Heather didn't have the time or money to worry about her wardrobe.

I ran after them. "Hey, where's your father?" I seem to have picked up this bad habit of letting words go directly out of my mouth without passing through my brain first. Sort of like agreeing to do the competition in the first place.

Heather stopped and looked at me strangely, as if her eyes were trying to dodge around mine and get into my head. But the pinched rat face was gone. She licked her lips and moved Suki to her other hip. The bunched-up folds of her black sweatpants made a great baby seat.

"He wasn't . . . dependable. So he, uh, left, right after Suki was born."

That didn't make sense to me, but I nodded.

Heather's eyes seemed to focus inward, and she kept going. "My mother was a concert violinist and a nurse. She couldn't decide which one she really wanted to do, so she had us. Some decision."

"Oh." I pictured a young Mrs. Bardlow in a Florence Nightingale nurse's cape, roving from hospital bed to hospital bed with her violin, healing patients with the sound of music.

"My father was a librarian, but he just didn't get it."

"Didn't get what?" I ventured.

"Life!" With a snap, the rodent was back, and Heather hugged Suki to her fiercely. We were perched midway down the narrow stairs. It was my turn to say something.

"A concert violinist," I said, trying to sound normal, but my voice squeaked. I wanted to pole-vault over the two of them and escape out the door, over the broken front porch while there was still time. "So that's where you get your musical talent."

"Hey! We need to practice!" Heather turned and went down the stairs, with Suki bouncing cheerfully on her hip.

Chapter **Seven**

It was a long walk home from Heather's house, but I needed the fresh air. We had made decent progress on the Kuhlau while Suki pulled all the pots and pans out of the kitchen cabinets. And we'd played the Beethoven together again. I could still feel the notes dancing around inside my head.

But something about Heather's house and the way she talked about her parents gave me the creeps. No wonder she was such a loner. Practicing with her was fun, but I wasn't so sure how I felt about spending the next month and a half with a hyperactive washing machine, apple-juicy floors, and that strange rat face. Why did I ask about her father? I really didn't need to know where he was. Mine wasn't around and it didn't matter—we were fine. Everything was fine.

No. Wait a minute. Everything was not fine. May 14th, the competition date, suddenly blared in my head like a foghorn. A month and a half away. Warning, warning! All hands on deck! The purple monsters started bouncing on my heart. *Think of a good excuse. I need a good excuse. How about: Heather is weird. Yeah, that works. Why head straight for the rocks? Run away! Run away!* All the way home my flute case banged on my leg like a shutter flapping in a storm.

I leaned over to unlock the front door. The more I thought about it, the more I liked the idea of quitting while I was ahead. I wouldn't have to give up playing the flute altogether. I could just stay away from Heather and wait awhile before going full-steam ahead with anything as big as a competition.

I tried not to think of how proud Dad had sounded when he told me to go for great.

"It wouldn't really be quitting, just trimming my sails," I told myself, sliding two chicken potpies into the hot oven just as Mom came through the door.

"Honey? Who are you talking to?"

Great. I was talking to the chicken potpies.

Heather's weirdness was already beginning to rub off on me.

"No one, Mom. Guess I'm just a little out of it today."

"Or lonely?"

She put her briefcase down and gave me a hug. "I think I've found a solution. There's an after-school club at Kids Plus. They do crafts and things—you know, like pottery, drama, cooking, stuff like that. And on Wednesdays there's a choral-sing." She pulled a brochure out of her coat pocket. "I signed you up for Mondays and Wednesdays. There's a special bus that will pick you up at school."

I slowly unfolded the pages. "Day care? Mom!"

"It's not day care, Jenna. Come on, honey, it's a club. You need to be with other kids. It'll be fun."

The Kids Plus logo was a laughing teddy bear.

"Mom!" Shocked tears were bubbling up inside me, ready to spill. I thought of Heather wrestling alone with the washing machine tube and fought the tears back. Suddenly even Heather's weird moods and sticky kitchen floor seemed better than making dumb clay things with a bunch of babies.

"You signed me up? You signed me up for Mondays and Wednesdays?! Did you ever think of asking me first? Well, I'm already busy, and it's not making clay ashtrays at the Laughing Bear!"

Mom opened her mouth.

I didn't let her say anything. "I told you about the competition, but you're so busy being 9-to-5 with Crunchy-Crispos that you didn't even hear me. Well, it's too late. It's none of your business what I'm doing on Mondays and Wednesdays, but I'm not, not, NOT going to day care!"

Finally the tears burst out. I ran to my room and slammed the door.

Chapter **Eight**

I was miserable. As soon as I had declared myself back in the competition, I was looking for some way out. Mom was living in Crunchy-Crispos world, Heather's mismatched socks and creepy house drove me crazy, and Caitlin was never around when I called.

The way life was going, I wasn't surprised at all when Michelle and Caitlin came up to me the next week at gymnastics looking all shy and excited— like they were going to announce their engagement or something.

Michelle flicked a curl and nudged Caitlin. "You tell her. She's *your* best friend."

"Tell me WHAT?" It came out louder than I

meant it to, and everybody in the gym turned to look at me. I tried to smile. "I mean, what's up?"

Caitlin looked like she was going to float up to the ceiling in heavenly bliss.

Michelle grabbed an imaginary microphone. "Now that you've made the gymnastics team, Caitlin Oliveira, what are you going to do next?"

Great. Michelle was stealing my friends and my jokes. Well, Cat was still my friend, and I was going to be happy for her whether I wanted to be or not. I threw my arms around her. "You made the team? That's great! When did you find out?"

"They just posted it. And, well . . . the only bad part is that I won't be in your class anymore."

I stepped back.

Caitlin nodded over to the group of older girls on the balance beam. "I mean, it's the same time, but a different class. We can still do Tuesdays and Thursdays together, see?"

Michelle chimed in helpfully, "We have practice four times a week."

"We?"

"Yeah. Me and Caitlin. I made the team, too. Our first meet's next month."

Caitlin didn't notice that my smile was frozen on my face. "I'm going to do a routine on the uneven bars. I can't wait!"

Caitlin kept bubbling all the way home about how great the gymnastics team was. They had won the state championship two years ago. She was going to ride in buses to meets all over the state. Maybe she would get a ribbon for the uneven bars in April. Maybe she'd get her picture in the paper.

I sighed.

Mrs. Oliveira looked at me over her glasses. "How's the Beethoven going, Jenna?"

"It's a lot of work, but at least it doesn't give me calluses."

Caitlin giggled and picked at hers. "Hey, who's that on your doorstep?" she asked, as we pulled into my driveway. It was Heather with her flute. I suddenly had the urge to use her as ammunition against Michelle. Like a counter-jealousy attack.

"It's Heather Bardlow. We practice together—every day."

"Every day?" A hint of jealousy. My plan was working.

"Well, not weekends."

"Every day with *Heather*?" The plan was not working. Caitlin wasn't jealous at all. She was just amazed that I could stand to spend that much time in the mismatched socks zone.

I gathered up my books and sweater. "Yeah, she's a really good musician."

"Well, I'm glad Heather Featherbrain is good at something."

Mrs. Oliveira glanced at Caitlin in the rearview mirror. "Caitlin, that's not nice."

"She is good," I said. "Maybe you could come listen to us . . . sometime." Maybe never, I hoped.

"Sure. Stay loose, goose."

I swung the car door closed. "Thanks, Mrs. O. Later, Cat."

So much for the counter-jealousy attack.

Heather didn't say anything to me when I came up the steps. She just blinked. So I opened the door without saying anything. I hated her for being such a social zero. Like me. Caitlin gets the new girl. I get the elf-rat.

But Heather *was* a good practice partner, no doubt about it. She loved the idea I had gotten the night before for phrasing the staccato run in the Handel *bourrée*. And she showed me how to do the grace notes, those little notes that bounce up and down next to the main melody notes. The trill was a killer though. I wanted to be able to make my flute warble like Heather's.

"My tongue feels like a jellyfish," I muttered.

Heather tapped her chin like she always does when she's thinking.

I rolled my tongue around inside my mouth. "I

can't move that fast. Should I tongue each note or do it all in one breath?"

"Try it real slow and see what happens."

By the end of the hour we hadn't conquered any of the tough parts or erased any circles, but we sure knew where they all were. Then Heather put the Beethoven on the music stand. "OK, let's see how this one's doing. Why don't you run through the first part. Like it's a performance."

She sat down on my bed, folded her hands, and turned her elf face up to me.

Like a performance. The bottom fell out of my stomach, and somebody else's arms picked up my flute and put it to my lips. The black notes floated up off the page and swarmed into my eyes like gnats. I blinked and the notes settled back onto the page. But now the music was upside down and backward! Air came out of my mouth, producing the first three notes, but then that was it. There was no more air in my lungs or anywhere in the room. Instead there was some kind of clear goo that made it really hard to move or breathe. I couldn't look at Heather. I sat down on the floor and laid my flute next to me.

"I can't do it. It's no use." I didn't feel my lips move, but I heard my voice.

I sat there in silence. Little by little, the air trickled back into the room. I could feel my lungs moving in and out, in and out. I finally lifted my head, expecting to see Heather's rat face snarling back at me.

But it wasn't. It was a face of sadness like I'd never seen before. There were tears in her eyes. She didn't move to brush them away. Her gaze was soft, but it locked on to mine.

"Never say that," she whispered. "Never, ever, ever say that."

After Heather left, I felt like crawling into bed and curling up in a tiny little ball. Instead I opted for a nice, long bubble bath. I poured bubbles into the water, slipped into the tub, and floated an imaginary bubble up into my brain, trying to keep everything else out. No thoughts now, thank you very much.

"I just want to go home." I stuck my big toe up into the faucet, the way I've always done since I was little. "But you are home, you big baby." *Right. And I'll be in a mental home if I keep having such stimulating conversations with myself.*

Mom was late getting home from work, which was good because it gave me a chance to finish my bath, get dressed, and make some dinner. I didn't have time for anything as fancy as lasagna, but I was able to make some ziti with canned sauce and put it in the oven with plenty of mozzarella cheese on top.

Mom was impressed when she came in. "Wow! Fine dining at Jenna's Italian Bistro!"

I smiled, but suddenly Caitlin's words, "Well, at least she's good at something," seeped into my head and popped that empty bubble. "Gee, thanks," I mumbled sarcastically.

"What was that, hon?" Mom pulled a thin line of melted cheese up over her head with her fork. "You've got the ratio of sauce to cheese down perfectly, Jen-girl."

"Nothing." I blinked and the bubble filled my head again. I concentrated on the mozzarella, but it hardly had any taste.

"How would you like to go on a business trip with me?" Mom suddenly asked.

"A what?" I pushed Heather's face out of my mind and tried to listen to my mother.

"There's an advertising convention in Chicago this spring. It's on a weekend, so you wouldn't miss any school. There's a fancy awards dinner that you could come to, and you could help hand out flyers at our booth in the convention hall. My boss says you could be our official intern. You wouldn't get paid, but they'd cover your flight and everything."

"Flight?" Now she had my attention. I loved flying. I even liked airplane food.

"Come on, honey. I think you'd have fun. And you'd be a big help."

I pictured myself looking important in a black tailored suit with a briefcase full of pamphlets and flyers. It did sound kind of fun.

I looked down at my ziti. "Do I have to dress up like a giant Crunchy-Crispo?"

"No!" Mom burst out laughing and flew around the table to give me a hug. She glanced at the calendar on the kitchen wall. "It's the weekend of May 14th and 15th."

The weekend of the competition. Mom had obviously forgotten. I was about to get mad when a purple fear monster stopped me. *Why not conveniently forget, too?* I thought. *Let's see. I could eat airplane food, wear cool clothes, and be an intern for an advertising company. Or I could stay home and humiliate myself in front of a whole auditorium full of people.*

"Sure. I'll go." Done. No more competition. That was that. Mom hugged me again. She was ecstatic. Why wasn't I?

Chapter **Nine**

I didn't have the heart to tell Heather I was bowing out of the competition, so I didn't tell her about the business trip. I just kept practicing with her. And I was starting to make progress, too. Funny. Now that I wasn't so worried about the competition, I was playing much better.

On Friday Heather left me a note in my locker, asking a strange question. I walked over to her desk before French class and read it back to her: "Can you play 'Three Blind Mice'?"

Ms. Buttner frowned at me. She hates it when we speak English in her classroom. Heather raised her eyebrows as if to say, "Well, can you?"

It took me a minute to remember how to say "But of course!" in French. "*Mais, bien sûr!*"

"May, byen sur," Ms. Buttner repeated, beaming. Heather gave me an elf smile and a wink.

I didn't think much of it until later that day when I was at the Petersons' babysitting and Heather showed up at the door. She had her flute in hand and Suki on her back in a baby carrier.

"A command performance for the two Grand Duchesses of Babyville," Heather announced, making her way into Meggie's playroom. She sat down and slipped the Suki-carrier off her back. She stood it up, with Suki still in it, on the floor next to one of Meggie's little chairs.

Then she bowed and kissed Meggie's hand. "Your Royal *Ex*-cellence, we would be *ex*-tremely honored if we could play you a song. Please be seated in your royal throne. The performance will begin shortly." Meggie giggled and sat down obediently.

Suki clapped and cheered. "Mmmee-mee-mee-MAAAA!"

Heather had already found my flute case by the door and was handing it to me. She leaned toward me and whispered, "They're loving us already! Quick, get your flute together."

I finally got around to closing my mouth.

When I was ready, Heather turned to our tiny

audience and bowed. "And now, for your listening enjoyment, we present 'Three Blind Mice.'"

She gave me the starting signal with a swing of her flute, and we both began to play.

"Again! Again!" shrieked Meggie as soon as we had finished.

This time we got fancy. I played the melody and Heather played a harmony with lots of little trills and runs. What a hit! We played the song about five more times and then moved on to "Old MacDonald," "Frère Jacques," and "Row, Row, Row Your Boat," which we did in a round.

Little Grand Duchess Meggie didn't mind that Heather's socks didn't match. Or that the hem of her plaid skirt was uneven. When it was time for Heather to leave, Meggie wrapped her arms around Heather's waist and cried, "Stay-y-y!"

Heather looked up at me from under her blond frizzles as she pried Meggie's little fingers off her skirt. "I guess your first concert was a success," she said.

So that's what this was all about. I laughed and swept Meggie up into my arms. Heather had tricked me into playing for an audience without being scared. No fear monsters. No heaving stomach. Just some fun with a couple of toddlers.

Now I wanted to hug Heather. This was like freedom. I grabbed her arm and looked into her face. This time there wasn't an elf or a rat or anything weird. It was just a girl's face. A face that wanted a friend. Wanted *me* for a friend.

I swallowed the lump in my throat and said, "Thanks."

On Saturday, we decided to take things to the next level. We would be wandering minstrels and serenade the whole neighborhood. *This is going to be fun,* I told myself as I got out of bed that morning. *Yeah, right,* my stomach gurgled back. I put on my Robin Hood hat with the long feather and made a funny face in the mirror. *Fun, fun, fun,* I repeated to myself. *Not, not, not,* sang my stomach. I wanted to go back to bed.

But when I answered the door, there was an elf with a huge plastic nose, bushy mustache, and thick black glasses standing on the front steps. I burst out laughing. Heather grinned and pointed to the fake nose and glasses. "Scientifically proven to reduce jitters." She swept off the disguise and put it in her back pocket. "For emergencies only," she warned.

We started out in my driveway, playing the Handel *bourrée.* The only audience was the mail carrier, who walked by and waved. My stomach waved back. I missed a note, but I thought of Heather in that silly disguise and kept on playing.

Then we took Beethoven and Kuhlau to the park. A mother with a baby asleep in his stroller sat smiling with her eyes closed through the whole Kuhlau *menuett,* even though I stumbled in three different places and almost wiped out on the dreaded staccato run. *Go away!* my brain yelled at the fear monsters. *Anything sounds good to this woman as long as it's not her baby crying.*

After that we had to walk around a little until my heart stopped slam-dancing and the feather in my Robin Hood cap stopped trembling. Then Heather pulled out the Beethoven. "The best for last," she grinned.

Two blue-haired ladies with huge pocketbooks and sensible walking shoes stopped to listen. When we finished, they applauded and chirped, "Bravo, bravo!"

My heart was pounding, but I swept off my hat in a grand bow. To my surprise, one of the ladies put a dollar in it.

The other started digging in her purse. She waved away our "No thank-you's" and pressed a crumpled-up dollar bill into Heather's hand.

We waited until they'd shuffled off before we cracked up.

"We're rich, we're rich!" I shrieked, waving my dollar in Heather's face.

"My first professional paycheck." Heather held the bill up to her cheek lovingly. "I'll never spend you," she declared.

"Not even at the Pizza Palace?" I asked. I felt like celebrating, even though my stomach would probably have been happier going home and having Tums for dinner. "The Saturday Special—a slice and a Coke for one dollar!" I waved the money temptingly.

Heather looked at her dollar and shrugged. "OK, I'll spend you on pizza."

The cheese was perfectly stringy. It hit the spot after a hard day of flute playing. I opened my mouth to take a bite and suddenly found myself talking instead. "It's not just jitters. I have really bad stage fright." There it was. Plopped out on top of my pizza like a smelly old anchovy. "Waiter, waiter," I wanted to yell, "I didn't order this."

But Heather just chewed and nodded. Maybe she didn't really understand. "I mean, I can't even move or breathe," I said.

Heather took a sip of Coke. "I used to get scared, too, when I played with my mom. We used to do a lot of concerts at the Y, and the library, and stuff." She wrinkled up her nose. "All those faces, looking at me—yikes!"

"So what did you do?"

"I made up little tricks, games to play in my head. You know, like these—" she patted the nose and glasses in her back pocket—"to take my mind off how nervous I felt."

I picked at my pizza crust. "Did you ever completely lose it while you were playing? I mean, totally panic and freeze up?"

Heather licked her fingers and leaned toward me. "No. See, what you do is pick one face in the audience, one that you trust, and play only for that person. Try not to even see anybody else. Block all the other people out."

"Hmmm."

Heather's eyes started focusing inward again. Like that day on the stairs when she told me that her father didn't "get it." I wondered if she was thinking about him again now. Wherever he was, he probably wasn't the face in the crowd she could trust. Heather's horrible rat face was coming back. I had to change the subject quickly.

"Want the rest of my pizza?" It was the only thing I could think of.

Heather blinked and the rat face was gone. "Sure." She reached over for it. "What I also used to do was try to curl and uncurl my toes while I was playing. Doesn't work if your shoes are too tight, though."

I laughed and nodded in agreement.

"Or how about this?" Heather started giggling. The elf face twinkled up at me. "You look out into the audience and pretend that everyone is sitting in their underwear. Over-*exposure.*"

"Their underwear!" I thought about Meggie's Muppet Baby underwear. I imagined our French teacher, Ms. Buttner, in a pair of Kermit underpants. Or what about our principal, Mr. D'Amato, in Miss Piggy boxers? Michelle Rafferty would look oh-so-special in her Sesame Street pull-ups. There they all were, sitting there in their glory. I started to laugh. The purple monsters didn't stand a chance against an audience full of underwear. Maybe—just maybe!

Chapter **Ten**

I was heading home from school on Wednesday, whistling the staccato run from the Kuhlau piece under my breath and trying to get the phrasing right. I didn't hear Caitlin come up behind me. "What are you mumbling, girl?"

"Huh?" I suddenly realized that I had stopped whistling and started chanting. Chanting "May 14th"! I sighed. The stress was catching up to me. I still hadn't pointed out to Mom that her convention was the same day as the competition. And after our concert in the park, how could I tell Heather I wasn't going to do the competition?

My face got hot, and I looked around. Bus kids

were piling onto the buses. Most of the walkers were running ahead of us, shouting, because it was such a beautiful day. Nobody seemed to be pointing at me and laughing at the weird girl chanting to herself.

Caitlin fell in step beside me. "Don't worry, I'm the only one who knows you're crazy." Her face got serious. "Where's Heather?"

"She had an appointment this afternoon. I'm meeting her later at the video arcade."

"Video arcade? I didn't realize that playing video games was part of your flute training." She laughed, but I could tell that something was bothering her.

"It's not. We're going there to practice. See, we've started playing in different places—like the arcade, the park, the train station—to get used to performing in front of people."

"Oh, like wandering minstrels? I get it. Hey, how come you missed gymnastics yesterday? Mom was all devastated that she didn't get to hum Mozart with you." Caitlin paused. "And you weren't home last night when I tried calling you."

I shrugged. "I just needed some more flute practice time. It's not exactly going to make or break my Olympic career if I miss gymnastics once in a while."

Caitlin grabbed her braid and started chewing the end of it. She does that when she's nervous, which isn't very often. Wow. The last time I saw her chew that hard was in third grade, right before our first book report. Something was definitely up. She spit out the braid.

"Don't you ever take a break from practicing? I mean, I'm glad you're doing the competition and everything, but what about me? I'm your best friend, and I hardly ever see you anymore." She stopped suddenly. "Why do you have to practice with Heather so much? Can't you take it on your own now? You must have practiced together enough by now."

"Caitlin, Heather's not that bad."

"Yeah, well, maybe there are things you don't know about her." Caitlin looked over her shoulder.

"Some things I don't know?" Probably things I didn't want to know. I started walking again. "Gee, it was nice talking to you, Caitlin. Maybe we can do something next Saturday," I said sarcastically, hoping to change the subject.

"Hey!" Caitlin grabbed my shoulder. "Listen!" No one was around, but she still lowered her voice to a whisper. "Heather's father was crazy. Schizophrenic. He killed himself."

One time I pulled open my desk drawer and the bottom fell out. All kinds of little bits and pieces of things landed on the floor. Pencil stubs, rubber bands, scraps of notepaper, a tiny magnifying glass, and the broken handle of an old baby rattle. It had all seemed so neat and orderly in the drawer, but suddenly it was just a pile of junk.

That's how I felt now. All my little worries and fears and hopes and plans. Just a bunch of junk.

I stared at Caitlin. "He killed himself? Why?"

"I don't know." Caitlin shifted uncomfortably. "He was crazy. And it could be in the genes, you know—inherited."

I thought of Heather morphing from elf to rat and wondered. "You think Heather's crazy?"

Caitlin nodded. "Jenna, I don't think you should play with her anymore." She sounded like she was about four years old, warning me not to make mud pies with the neighborhood troublemaker. But she was serious.

"Caitlin, I'm sure it's not catching."

Caitlin shuddered. "Maybe not. But it's just not—well, cool."

That didn't sound like Caitlin at all. Since when did Caitlin worry about being cool? Then I remembered Michelle snickering in the music room.

Heather was waiting for me at the video arcade. I had been really nervous about this performance because the arcade is where the eighth graders hang out. But as it turned out, I didn't have time to be nervous. I was too busy trying not to let Heather know what was running around in my head. *Did he hang himself? Shoot himself? Did Heather find him? Please no, not that. Where did it happen? Was he angry and mean? Or just confused?*

We set up our music stand in front of a soda machine near the snack bar. I couldn't look at Heather, so I pretended to be busy looking through the sheet music. The Beethoven piece fell onto the floor.

"Perfect choice," Heather said, picking it up and dusting it off. We started playing. I must have been on automatic pilot because I don't remember thinking about the notes. I was wondering how Heather was able to laugh at anything anymore. All around us video machines beeped and whirred, pinball flippers clacked, and the virtual kick-boxing game gave off imitation groans and grunts. I wondered if people who committed suicide went to hell, and if they did, whether it would sound like this.

Someone lit a cigarette. The sudden fumes made me choke, but I kept playing. As I glanced up, I saw some kids with weird haircuts wander by. They were dressed mostly in black. The guy with the cigarette was one of them. He was wearing black nail polish. He looked like he was trying to do an impression of a dead person. A girl with green hair and a black leotard followed close behind him. There was something about her that reminded me of Michelle. But it couldn't be Michelle. Michelle was at gymnastics doing perfect vaults, flirting with the instructors, and stealing my best friend while I was playing Beethoven in a scuzzy arcade, trying to figure out what to say to a friend whose father had committed suicide.

The piece was finished. I was standing there, motionless, with my flute up to my lips.

Heather nudged me. "Hey, you. It's over. We did it! If we can play here, we can play anywhere." She smiled and gave me the thumbs up. "You did great. We'll get those purple monsters."

I made myself look at her and smile back. "Yeah, yeah." Compared to Heather's demons, my purple monsters seemed like Easter candy.

I stepped into my house and just stood there, numb. The phone was ringing. I walked over to it and answered it, as if that was exactly what I was planning to do.

A wave of static hit my ear. Like putting your ear up to a seashell. Like a ship-to-shore radio!

"Dad!"

"Jenna, you're home! I know it's not Friday night, but I had a chance to call you so I thought I'd take it."

"I miss you, Daddy. Where are you?"

"Halfway round the world—" A surge of crackling interference swept his voice away. I squeezed the receiver to my ear, like that would somehow bring his voice back. It did.

"—modern technology, right here!"

I didn't care where he was. I just wanted to hear his voice. "Uh-huh."

"How's your music coming?" he asked.

"OK, Dad. But sometimes . . ."

"Didn't read that. Come over again?"

"Nothing, Dad."

"You know, when I'm out here on the bridge polishing the chrome, I think of you polishing every note of your music."

"Dad, officers aren't supposed to be *polishing*."

"Jenna, a good sailor can't help it. It's an insurance policy. If something on a ship's not polished, it might not be shipshape. If it's not shipshape, it might be broken. If something on a ship's broken, what's going to come between a sailor and the sea? A polished ship is a safe ship."

I giggled. "Polished notes are safe notes."

Dad laughed, too, and the static crested. "That's the spirit. Just pay attention to the details, one by one, while they're small enough to handle, and you'll be making good headway."

"Heather says once you know all the notes, you can start to learn the *music*."

"Heather sounds like a smart girl. Glad to hear you've got a new friend."

He said something else, but the crackling connection drowned him out.

"I can't hear you!" I shouted into the phone.

From very far away, as the static ebbed and flowed, I heard him shout again.

"I love you, too, Daddy!" But the line was already dead.

Chapter **Eleven**

The next day I was in the gym running laps with Caitlin and Michelle, killing time before gymnastics. Michelle was wearing a silver-blue leotard with little sparkly things sewn up and down the sleeves and along the neckline. It was low cut, and it made her look about eighteen.

Caitlin was trying to sell Michelle on the idea of Gram's inn.

"Why would we want to go *there*?" Michelle snorted. I guess she was too mature for sleepovers.

"We can build a fire in the fireplace and stay up really late and watch videos," Caitlin panted as we rounded the corner behind the uneven bars.

"All of the beds have canopies," I added. Convincing Michelle to come was the last thing I wanted to do, but I wasn't going to let anyone think that Gram's inn was dorky.

"And we get to go horseback riding!" Caitlin continued.

I could almost smell the warm, wonderful animal smell. I really needed a weekend away. Away from flute playing, stomachaches, latchkey land, and Mom's Crunchy-Crispos. Away from Heather and her horrors. The idea of snuggling up with Michelle for the weekend didn't thrill me, but it was better than not going at all. If Caitlin liked her, there must be something good about her. Maybe I just had to get to know her.

We stopped at the Tumble Trak and started jogging in place to cool down. "I'm glad you're here," Caitlin whispered in my ear. "You know, not with Heather."

"Are there any guys at Gram's inn?" asked Michelle.

Caitlin looked over at me mischievously. "Oh yeah. Alfie would go for you in a second, Michelle," she said.

"Who's Alfie?" Now Michelle was interested.

We plopped down on the floor to do some stretching exercises.

"Alfie's the stable hand," I explained, playing along with Caitlin's joke. "A real dreamboat. He has the most incredible blue eyes."

"Mmm-hmm," Caitlin added, sighing dreamily.

Alfie was about ninety-four years old. He chewed tobacco and washed his hair maybe once a year. He did have nice eyes, though.

It was like the old days with Caitlin again, playing jokes and being silly. I happily jumped onto the Tumble Trak to work on my rotten Russian straddle. I had forgotten my leotard, so I was wearing one of Caitlin's. It made me feel like her. I almost felt lighter. I tried moving my arms the way she does. I was bouncing higher and higher, pointing my toes like a real gymnast. I could feel every muscle in my body.

Suddenly the Russian straddle made sense. My legs lifted in a perfect *V,* and there it was. Finally I could do it! Caitlin and Michelle even noticed from the balance beam.

Caitlin ran over, waving her hands and grabbing an imaginary microphone. "Now that you've mastered the Russian straddle, Jenna Dowling, what will you do next?"

I grinned and bounced up one more time. We both thought of it at the same time and shouted, "Why, go to Gram's inn, of course!"

My legs were still tingling with excitement from the Russian straddle as I walked to the commuter train station to meet Heather. And I needed all the positive vibrations I could get. Today's goal was to play the Kuhlau piece—including the staccato run—during rush hour. It was a warm day, and the forsythia were starting to turn from yellow to green. I tried to concentrate on counting the yellow flowers instead of counting the number of flips my stomach was making. I really didn't want to do the Kuhlau in front of so many people until I had mastered the staccato run.

"Relax," said Heather. "Eighty-three percent of these people have no idea how it's supposed to sound. The other sixteen percent are only thinking about getting home."

"Seventeen percent."

"Well," Heather said, smirking, "probably there's one percent who will be paying attention to exactly–how–precise–each–of–those–staccato–notes–is!" She pinched her thumb and finger in little dit-dits as she said each word.

"Great." My stomach oozed. "I'll just set my nerve-ometer for one percent."

But as it turned out, I never had to worry about

the staccato run. Before we'd even gotten to the second page, a bunch of older-looking kids dressed mostly in black, with pierced noses, lips, and eyebrows, walked by and hovered behind Heather. They were the kids from the arcade. What were they doing here? I turned toward Heather a little to keep an eye on them. One of them, a big kid with a bandanna, nudged the girl next to him and pointed at Heather.

"That the one?" he asked.

The girl nodded and started pulling him away. She flung her hair in a nervous little dip. I knew that dip. It was Michelle! And then I realized it had been Michelle at the arcade, too, with the green hair. Her hair wasn't green now. It was ironed straight and her face was painted pale, almost white. She was wearing black lipstick, a black lace blouse over a black bra, and a black miniskirt. This outfit made the silvery blue leotard look innocent. I almost swallowed a dotted eighth note, but I kept on going.

Bandanna-head put his hand up to his mouth in a stage whisper, turning to his friends. "Tell her not to go too *crazy* with that flute. Wouldn't want her to end up schizo, like poor old Dad!"

Michelle's startled eyes caught mine. She gulped and smiled sheepishly, then took off like a bat flapping out of a nightmare before Heather could see her. My flute screeched to a halt. Heather's sounded like air hissing slowly out of an old tire. Bandanna-head and the rest of his friends just stood there, chuckling. Someone started to scream. It was me.

"Get out of here, you losers! Leave us alone! You don't know anything. YOU oughta have YOUR heads examined!"

The black bandits staggered off. A train arrived and filled the station with swishing legs. Heather let her flute drop to her side.

I put my arm around her. She felt stiff and cold. We stood there a little while. Commuters darted around us like fish around a sunken ship.

Finally Heather said, "He's not schizophrenic. He's dead."

I nodded. I sent a silent thank-you to Caitlin for telling me about this already.

"He was never schizophrenic. He was manic-depressive. Now the doctors call it bipolar. It's a mood disorder marked by extremes of excitement and depression," Heather recited wearily.

The *ex* words stabbed into me. I started to cry. I knew what she was going to say next, and I didn't want to hear it.

"He hated taking his medicine, and he killed

himself." Heather looked up at me. She wasn't crying. She was old and drained.

At that moment, I hated Heather's father even more than I hated Michelle. How could he do that to her? "But what about you?" I asked.

Heather misunderstood. She thought I was asking if she was crazy, too. "Well, it is genetic," she sighed. "But there are drugs you can take. So far, the doctors say I'm—" she twisted her mouth into a grimace, "—normal. But it's hard. I have to go for counseling at the hospital where my mother works." She looked up at the big station clock. "That's where I'm going now."

We packed up our flutes, and I walked her to the platform. Heather turned to me and tried to smile. "Thank you for being a friend," she said.

The train came, the doors opened, and Heather disappeared inside them.

Chapter **Twelve**

I was really late getting back. Mom was already home, and she was worried.

What could I say? "Gee, Mom, my best friend's new best friend, who I thought could have been my friend, too, was at the train station wearing black lipstick and hanging around with a bunch of creeps who made fun of my real friend, whose manic-depressive father killed himself. So then, I had to walk her to her train because I didn't want her to be too upset on her way to psychotherapy. By the way, the manic-depressive thing—it's a mood disorder and it's genetic."

I don't think so.

Instead all I said was, "Sorry, Mom."

But Mom wasn't just worried. She was mad. She flung a plate of canned stew onto the table.

"The librarian called with a book you reserved a week and a half ago. She says she can't hold it any longer." Mom's face was flushed.

My hand flew up to my mouth. "The science report! It's due tomorrow! I was gonna work on it last Saturday." How could school have the nerve to continue, with dead fathers, working mothers, competition dates, mood disorders, and fake friends in black lipstick zinging around in my head like crazed killer bees?

"Now that I've finally managed to make sense of my own calendar, I think we need to sit down and talk about yours," Mom said angrily. "I spoke to your father today, and he pointed out a little conflict I overlooked about a certain upcoming date known as May 14th." She threw her plate and fork into the dishwasher, scooped up a laundry basket full of dirty clothes, and dashed down the hall to the laundry room.

I sighed. Mom was probably madder at herself than at me, but I wasn't making things any easier for her. Laundry was supposed to be my job. The phone rang, and I pushed the stew away. It smelled like dog food. Caitlin was on the phone.

"Hey, Jenna, I just got home from gymnastics. Wanna meet me at the mall in an hour?"

"I can't. I have to work on my science report. It's due tomorrow!" I groaned.

Caitlin was determined. "OK, then how about tomorrow night? I'm sure Mr. Zandler will give you an extension. We'll walk to the library tomorrow after school, and I'll help you do the report. Then we can hit the mall."

"I can't. I've got Meggie Peterson tomorrow. I'm meeting Heather there to rehearse."

There was this big awful silence.

"Heather? But, I . . . I thought you were done with Heather."

I didn't know what to say.

Caitlin suddenly blurted out, "What about *me*? What about friends since kindergarten? I hardly ever get to see you anymore!"

I couldn't believe my ears. What about *me*? *What about Michelle!* I wanted to say. *You're usually busy enough with her.* The words were on the tip of my tongue, but I swallowed them. I wondered if Caitlin and Michelle had had a fight. Had Caitlin found out about Michelle's black lipstick and pierced-face friends? I hoped not. Caitlin would be stunned. And crushed. Black lipstick was definitely not her style.

I really missed Caitlin. I wished we were back in first grade again, when our biggest problem was finding perfectly flat stones for hopscotch. Now here we were in sixth grade, with Caitlin on the gymnastics team and me going for great in the Annual Lakeville College Competition for Instrumental Soloists. And I definitely couldn't skip out on Heather tomorrow. Not after what had happened at the train station. I shuddered.

I tried to take deep breaths, like Mr. Thompson's breathing exercises. "Caitlin, you're still my best friend. You *know* that. But I have to rehearse."

"Yeah, I understand. You're ditching me for a psycho."

"I am not!"

"OK, then you're ditching me for your flute."

"Caitlin!"

"You're *not* my best friend. People don't ignore their best friends. I hope you and your flute are very happy together!"

I couldn't take it anymore. "Well I hope you and *Michelle* are happy together. Why don't you just go ask her to be your best friend!"

"Fine. I *will*."

"Well, FINE!" I shouted into the phone.

"FINE!" she shouted back and hung up.

I slammed the phone down so hard that Mom

jumped. She was standing in front of me with a load of clean underwear. She didn't look mad anymore. She looked horrified.

"What was *that?*"

"Just my *ex*-best friend," I squeaked. My heart was pounding, and my throat felt like it had a boa constrictor wrapped around it. Mom put down the laundry and reached her arms out to me. I burst into tears.

I told Mom everything. I told her about Heather's father, Michelle's big fake act with Caitlin, her nasty friends at the train station, and finally about my stage fright. About wanting and not wanting to do the competition.

I was still schnorkling and sniffling when she got up to make me some tea and toast. She dumped the plate of stew into the sink. "This smells like dog food," she said.

I giggled.

She popped some bread into the toaster. "Well, honey, you have to make your own decision, but I think you should skip my convention and stick with your original plan. We can call the Petersons and see if you can stay with them for the weekend. I'm sure Meggie would love to have a sleepover!"

Great. So Meggie was taken care of. But what about me? "Mom?"

"Hmmm?"

"Did you ever have stage fright?"

"Well, once I had to accompany the glee club on the piano at a homecoming pep rally. I didn't even look at the music until the day before, so I hadn't really learned it. I was terrified. Of course, that wasn't stage fright, that was stupidity." Mom sat down and passed a cup of orange tea to me. "But you can be really well prepared for something and still be scared—that's natural. Sometimes it's good to be a little nervous. Keeps you on your toes."

I sipped my tea.

"So what happened? Did you play the songs?"

Mom laughed. "Sort of. After the first one, my friends in the glee club all sang really loudly so you couldn't hear any of the wrong notes I hit. Thank heaven for good friends!" She spread apricot jam on the toast and cut it into triangles like she used to when I was little. "But here's what my grandma Curtis always used to say," she continued. "'This, too, shall pass.' In other words, pretty soon it will all be over—shaky knees, boiling stomach, wrong notes—and you'll be able to look back and say, 'Hey, I did it, and I'm still here to tell about it!'"

I sipped more tea and looked at the orange-coated triangles. Color-coordinated tea and toast. I had to hand it to Mom.

"Think of it this way, sweetie. What's the worst that could happen?"

I wanted to say, "The room will fill up with a gelatinous goo designed to stop my airflow. Tiny black dots will begin to stab at my eyes, and two huge purple things will drown me in a giant tidal wave."

Instead I said, "Right, Mom. What's the worst that could happen?"

Chapter **Thirteen**

Mr. Zandler did give me an extension on the science report. "I'm sure you must be very busy preparing for the Lakeville College competition," he said, stacking a pile of microscope slides. "I hear you're one of Franklin's finest flutists."

Did the whole school know my life story? And was I in the competition or wasn't I? Mom and Mr. Zandler seemed to think I was. But *I* wasn't so sure. I gulped. Then I tried curling my toes in my shoes. It didn't help.

"Well, first I have to make it through the preliminaries. But thanks, Mr. Zandler. I'll hand the report in to you first thing Monday morning."

I waved my notebook at him and zoomed off.

Caitlin totally ignored me that day, not to mention the whole weekend and the next week. But amazingly, Heather seemed pretty much back to normal. Or at least she pretended she was. We never discussed the train station. And we just slowly stopped doing the concerts. It was getting too rainy out anyway.

We started playing the pieces from memory, and that's when I really began to pull my hair out. I could play all the hard parts now—I had even erased my last circles around the Kuhlau staccato run. But the music didn't make sense to me anymore. Just a bunch of notes flung together. Even the Beethoven felt stale. A big so-what.

Then, one day after school, Heather and I arrived at my house to find Caitlin and Michelle waiting for us on the front step. My mouth dropped open.

Caitlin flipped her braid over her shoulder like nothing had ever happened. "We're skipping gymnastics today and going to the mall. Want to come with us?" she asked, putting her arm around my shoulder as if we were the same old best friends again.

I didn't know how to react. I wasn't sure I was ready to sweep the whole fight under the rug. But

I had to admit it was a relief to have her talking to me again.

Michelle was wearing her sexy black leotard with an old pair of jeans. She had that pale makeup on again, but with soft pink lipstick. She actually looked kind of pretty. She tried to smile a real smile. But I knew she was wondering what I was thinking. Her eyes darted nervously to Heather.

"She can come too," Michelle said.

Heather started whistling Beethoven. Her hem was coming undone in the back, and her shirt was hanging out. She looked so goofy. I was getting sick of Beethoven. I suddenly wished Heather would shut up.

Three more weeks till the competition. Three more weeks of being trapped in a room with Beethoven, Kuhlau, Handel—and Heather.

Caitlin was picking at her calluses. I could tell she needed a break from gymnastics as much as I needed a break from rehearsing.

I sighed and turned to Heather. "Come on, it'll be fun!"

Heather's mouth was a thin line. "I'd love to, but I don't *skip* practicing."

Caitlin rolled her eyes. Steam was going to pour out of my ears any second. I grabbed Heather's elbow and steered her to the curb as she hissed at me, "I thought we were doing the competition together."

I felt like shouting, but I kept my voice low. "We are! But I need a break. Music isn't the only thing in my life, you know. I happen to need friends, too. You could stand a few extra friends yourself, Heather Featherbr—" I clapped my hand over my mouth, but it was too late.

Heather's eyes filled with tears as she pulled away from me. She took a long strangled breath and drew herself up. "I hope your mall experience is absolutely *ex-quisite*!"

"I'll see you tomorrow," I called to Heather as she hurried off, but I don't think she heard me.

Caitlin shrugged her shoulders, and Michelle tossed her hair. The three of us headed slowly toward the mall. I decided I would get Heather something nice there. Maybe a mug that said "You're the best. I'm a jerk."

The mall was great, even though I was still feeling guilty. And even though Michelle was there. At one point, while Caitlin was in a dressing room trying on clothes, Michelle touched my elbow. Her voice was so soft I almost didn't recognize it.

"You know that day at the train station?" she

asked. "Well, um, thanks for not bringing it up. I didn't mean for those guys to be such jerks. I guess they can act kind of stupid sometimes."

"So why do you hang out with them?"

"I don't know. They're friends with my older brother, and I thought they were cool. I was just trying to—well, impress them, I guess, when I told them about Heather's dad. I didn't think they'd actually say anything to her. I mean, Heather is weird, but it's not her fault her dad—you know."

My mouth dropped open. "*Heather's* weird? And green hair *isn't*?"

"Yeah, well," Michelle smiled and struck a model's pose. "Call me a slave to fashion." She waited for me to laugh. I didn't. She looked down and kept talking. "Anyway, you're a really good flute player. I could never do what you do—playing in front of all those people. I'd get so nervous."

I thought of gymnastics. I thought of all the practices and competitions, with everybody looking at one girl alone on two uneven parallel bars. And suddenly I understood the flashy leotards, the black lipstick, and the big talk. Michelle was fighting her own purple monsters.

I grinned. "Well, what you do is, you imagine that everyone who's watching is in their underwear. Especially Scott Anderson!"

Michelle snorted, and we both cracked up.

Just then Caitlin burst out of the dressing room with her socks stuffed down the front of her dress. "How do you like my new *development*?" she giggled.

That's when we really lost it. Michelle was laughing so hard tears were streaming down her face. "Development!" she gasped. I laughed until it hurt.

We all stuffed ourselves with double fudge-mint sundaes. *Du glace.* I suddenly felt empty. *I'll see Heather tomorrow in French class,* I promised myself. *She'll be fine.*

But the next day she wasn't in French class. I didn't see her in school anywhere, in fact. At lunch I stopped by the office. Mrs. Renkin, our school secretary, was her usual perky self.

"Hello, Jenna. How's the flute playing coming along? I've heard all about the competition you're in!" She leaned forward, lowering her voice. "And teaming up with Heather Bardlow—that was nice of you. It's done wonders for that poor child."

Some teammate I was. Guilt settled in me like a sinking elevator going all the way down to the basement.

"Actually, Mrs. Renkin, speaking of Heather, could you tell me if she's out sick today?"

Mrs. Renkin pulled her glasses off to study the

list. "Bardlow . . . Bardlow. Yes! Here it is. She's absent today."

I decided I would call Heather as soon as I got home from gymnastics that afternoon. But when I picked up the phone to dial her number, Caitlin was on the line.

"That's magic, Jenna! Great minds think alike."

So I agreed to meet Caitlin at the library instead and never got around to calling Heather. Maybe a couple of days away from her and my flute would be good for us both.

On Friday I skipped lunch and sneaked out of the cafeteria to look for Heather. I knew she was in school somewhere. Mrs. Renkin told me she had seen her come in late. I checked the music room and the library before I thought of looking in the auditorium. When I got there, the lights were off, but I could see something small on the huge stage.

"Heather?"

She didn't answer, but I knew it was her. I started walking down the long aisle.

"I'm really sorry about everything. There's still plenty of time to practice together if you still want."

"Yeah, plenty of time." She spit out my words like they tasted sour. Then she held up her arm.

As I came closer, I could see something on her left wrist. A splint!

"What happened?"

"I fell down the stairs."

"NO WAY!" I ran the rest of the way down to the stage.

"It's not broken, just sprained. My mom says I'll be fine in two weeks," Heather said flatly.

"Two weeks?!"

"So I guess you'll have plenty of time to spend with your *friends* instead of with some stupid *featherbrain* like me," she said.

The rat face was back.

"Heather . . ." I started to walk toward her, but she got up and ran off the stage, out the back way. I heard the door slam behind her.

I looked out over the empty auditorium. What if Heather couldn't play in the competition now? It just wouldn't be fair!

That night I practiced for three hours.

On Saturday morning I was on Heather's doorstep with my flute and a pint of buttercrunch ripple. I pushed the ice cream at her before she could close the door.

"*Du glace.* For you! Guaranteed to heal sprained wrists five times faster than the leading cough syrup."

Heather gave in and opened the door with her elbow.

It was a rainy day, cold for spring. Heather's mother was home, cutting up carrots for soup. We set up the music stand in the kitchen. Heather couldn't bend her wrist to hold her flute, so she just stood beside me and watched. I could feel the electricity from her eyes boring into my fingers, almost flowing into the music. I watched the back of Mrs. Bardlow's head bobbing in time to her carrots and my notes. The kitchen filled up with soupy steam, but the music around us was perfectly clear.

When I got home the phone was ringing.

"Jenna?" I recognized Caitlin's voice.

"Hey, Caitlin! What's up?"

"Guess what—the date's been set!"

"What date?"

"Our weekend at Gram's inn."

"Oh, great! When?"

"Friday to Sunday, May 13th to the 15th."

"Caitlin. That's not even funny. When really?"

"That's it, Jenna. You're not worried about being there on Friday the 13th, are you? I think that's the best part! It's lucky 13 for us. Mark your calendar. Prepare your popcorn."

"My calendar *is* marked, Caitlin! That's the weekend of the flute competition—May 14th!"

"Ohhhhh, shoot—I forgot!" Caitlin groaned. "That's the only weekend Gram can give us."

"You're kidding," I sighed. Life was definitely not fair.

"Well, do you *have* to do the competition? I thought it was still a big maybe," Caitlin said.

"Yeah. I guess it is." I leaned my head against the kitchen wall. Why did there have to be so many better things to do on May 14th? I could be flying to Chicago. I could be staying at Gram's inn. But instead I would be "going for great." Or would I?

Chapter **Fourteen**

A week and a half later it was time for preliminaries. No big deal. Just play one of the three pieces for Mr. Thompson and the rest of the flute class. Except we were having class in the auditorium. Have I mentioned how *huge* our auditorium is?

"The chance to practice in here will give you an advantage," said Mr. Thompson, "because this is where the competition will be. The judges will sit up here," he pointed to the left side of the stage, "and you'll stand over there."

I suddenly had to go to the bathroom.

Mr. Thompson smiled. "Go ahead, Jenna. We'll wait for you."

I ran.

I locked myself into the stall. I closed my eyes. The floor rocked under my feet. Nope, I wasn't going to do it. I wasn't going to be judged because I wasn't going to play. Instead I was going to be nice and safe up at Gram's inn, eating popcorn, riding in horse-drawn buggies, and learning to fling my hair around like Michelle.

The girls' room door creaked open.

A very quiet voice said, "You don't have to go first. It's alphabetical."

Heather was standing outside my stall. Her wrist was still sore, but it had healed enough for her to play. It was stronger than I was. I knew I had to tell her about my decision, but I couldn't bring myself to do it face to face. So I stayed in the stall.

"I'm not doing the competition," I answered from behind the door. "I'm going out of town that weekend. There's this huge advertising convention in Chicago and then a party at Gram's inn."

Heather didn't seem surprised. She sighed. "OK, so you're out of town that weekend. But you're only in the bathroom right now. At least make it through the preliminaries. Then quit."

I opened the door slowly.

"I didn't really have to go to the bathroom," I said.

Heather nodded. "I know." She held out her arm to me.

I took it.

When we got back to the auditorium, Mr. Thompson asked Heather to play the Beethoven. She made it sound like a weepy Russian folk song. The rain of it was still falling on me when I was called up to the stage.

Mr. Thompson's voice floated out to me in the empty auditorium. "Jenna Dowling will play a *menuett* by Friedrich Kuhlau."

I forgot all about the Muppet underwear trick and totally blew the staccato run. But I played the rest of it pretty well. I could tell by Mr. Thompson's shining face.

"Brava! Brava!" He stroked his beard. "Congratulations, girls. We'll see you both a week from Saturday." Why was everybody so sure about that except me?

For the next week and a half, Heather talked Mr. Henderson, the school janitor, into unlocking the auditorium after school so we could practice in there. I told myself I was just going along to keep Heather company, but the truth was, playing in the auditorium was kind of fun. I got used to the way the big hall swallowed up the sound. And I learned to leave more time for the staccato notes in the

Kuhlau run. By Wednesday I could play the thing backward and forward.

Meanwhile, Heather was turning the Handel into circus music. She could make music say whatever she wanted it to, and when she played the *bourrée*, it said clowns and acrobats and prancing ponies. It made me want to dance up and down the aisles.

As the date of the competition got closer, Heather became a fireball. Her flute seemed to flash with lightning, and her hair practically stood on end, sizzling with sparks. She was awesome. Who cared if her socks didn't match?

"Brava! Brava!" I cried, stroking an imaginary beard. I couldn't wait for her to win a prize at the competition.

On Friday Heather suggested we have an unofficial dress rehearsal, and I agreed. Unofficially, of course. We invited Caitlin, Michelle, and some other kids.

I offered to go first. I figured I'd rather be the warm-up for Heather than have to follow her amazing act.

Caitlin announced way too formally, "Jenna Dowling will play Friedrich Kuhlau's *menuett*."

I got up and walked up the steps to the stage. My body felt like it was trying to float away, but I concentrated on putting one foot in front of the other. My black shoes looked like arrows on the red carpeted stairs.

Caitlin and Heather were waiting for me up on the stage. They nodded to each other in a judge-like way. I curled and uncurled my toes a couple of times and looked down at Michelle sitting in the front row. She licked her lips nervously. I suddenly realized she was nervous for *me*! The knobby head of a purple fear monster started pushing its way into my stomach. Where did that come from? I thought I was over that. Panic began to rise in my chest.

I took a deep breath. I made myself think of the tumbling notes in the staccato run, one by one. They were still there, clean and firm in my mind. Then I knew what to do. I looked straight at Michelle. I was going to say something to her with Friedrich Kuhlau's music. I was going to use it to wash both our fears away. True, clear music would wipe everything clean. I would stop worrying about the notes and concentrate on what I was trying to tell Michelle. Play the music, not the fear.

My knees were still wobbling, but my arms felt strong and sure as I brought my flute up to my lips. I smiled at Michelle. Then all I remember is that everything seemed to fit. I tossed out the staccato notes like jugglers' balls. They flipped off the far wall in perfect bounces. I did it. Everything was washed clean.

At first nobody said anything. Then Heather came over and hugged me. Michelle and the others started clapping. They were surprised. They were surprised I could play so well!

"I can do this. I can actually do this!" I shouted breathlessly.

Finally, all the hours of practicing were worth it. I was walking on air. I was floating on music. And I knew exactly where I wanted to be on Saturday, May 14th. Not in Chicago, not at Gram's inn. I would be competing in the Annual Lakeville College Competition for Instrumental Soloists.

Chapter **Fifteen**

On Saturday morning of the big day, Mom had tears in her eyes when she kissed me good-bye and got in the taxi to go to the airport.

"Here's the deal, Jen-girl," she said, trying to sound businesslike. "You blow 'em away at the competition, and I'll bring home the Crunchy-Crispos account, OK? Then, on Sunday night we can have a victory party! I'll save all the airplane peanuts for it."

"Thanks, Mom." I gave her a big hug and felt amazingly grown-up as I watched the taxi drive away.

Those grown-up feelings melted fast when I turned toward the house and realized that the front door had closed. I didn't have my key. I wasn't even dressed yet. My heart started pounding and my knees started shaking.

I was about to run shrieking down the street in my bathrobe yelling, "Mo-m-m-y-y-y!" but luckily I gave the doorknob a try first. The door was unlocked. As I fell into the house, laughing with relief, the phone was ringing.

"Flutes R Us!" I sang into the receiver.

Heather didn't even say hello. "Jenna, forget the whole thing. First my wrist, and now this." Her voice cracked.

"Now what, Heather? *What?!*"

"My mom was stuck at the hospital overnight with an emergency. She's still not home. I can't leave Suki alone. You're gonna have to go to the competition without me."

"No way, Heather! I'm sure we can find somebody to watch Suki." I couldn't believe this was happening.

"Like who? Your mom's in Chicago. Hey, what about Caitlin or Michelle?"

For a fleeting moment, I thought of Mom's comment, "Thank heaven for good friends." But then I remembered mine were at Gram's inn.

Do Not Panic, I told myself sternly.

"Isn't there anyone *you* can call?" I asked.

"I have an aunt in Wrentham, but she'd have to take the bus."

"OK. You call her." I glanced at the clock above the phone. Time was ticking away. Next to the clock was a note with our next-door neighbor's phone number on it. Mom had put it there for emergencies. "Mrs. Shimamura! I'll try her while you call your aunt." This was definitely an emergency.

Mrs. Shimamura wasn't home. Great. It was a good thing I wasn't bleeding to death. Then again, at least you can call an ambulance if you're bleeding to death.

I also tried the Petersons, but no one answered. They weren't expecting me at their house until dinnertime. I picked up the phone again and dialed Heather. Maybe her aunt was already on her way.

"Any luck?" I asked hopefully.

"No. Aunt Karen's in bed with the flu. She'd never make it here in time anyway. What about Mrs. Shimamura?"

"Not home. Neither are the Petersons." My stomach dropped. *What's the worst that could happen,* Mom had joked. This! This was the worst that could happen. Worse than purple monsters.

For the first time since this whole thing began, I really wanted to play in the competition. I had practiced, I was good, and I wanted to be great.

I wanted to stand up, all alone, and play my flute in front of everyone. So it wasn't easy for me to say what I said next:

"Heather, bring Suki over here. I'll watch her while you're at the competition."

"No! That is not an option." Heather was suddenly back in charge. "I'm going to see if Mr. Peterson is over at the playground with Meggie. Otherwise . . ."

"Otherwise what?!"

"I've got another idea. Just stall till I get there."

The hallway in front of the auditorium was abuzz. An iron-haired woman sat at the doorway checking off names.

"No. Absolutely no parents," she was telling a boy clutching a clarinet. "Only musicians are allowed inside." She had a long, thin nose and a sharp pencil. The boy was in high school, but he looked like he was about to cry.

I stepped up to the check-in table. "Ma'am? My friend might be a little late. Her mother . . ." My words wilted under her glare. I gave her my name and slipped inside, praying she wasn't a judge.

The auditorium was a sea of bobbing instruments, as kids held them up in the air to make their way to their seats. We filled the rows by grade. The sixth graders had to sit way down in front because we would be performing first. The rows behind me were slowly filling up. In front of me the stage was empty, except for the American flag and a table for the judges. The echoey sounds buzzing all around made me feel like I was in a dream. The huge walls started leaning in toward me, and my stomach began to burble.

Cory Banstable sat down two seats over, clutching her violin. Cory and I had been in the fourth grade together. She used to love laughing at really stupid knock-knock jokes. She wasn't laughing now. She looked like she was about to throw up.

"Too many people," she croaked. "I've never felt like this before."

I nodded. "Welcome to the club."

There *were* too many people. This was going to be one long competition. If only the sixth grade could go last—then Heather would have plenty of time. And I would have a chance to calm my stomach down. Or go to the bathroom and throw up.

Suddenly Cory was thrusting her violin and bow at me. She ducked her head down between her legs and started panting. *Perfect,* I thought. *Two sickies and no Heather.*

I put my flute and Cory's violin on the floor and

slipped into the seat next to her. She wasn't throwing up, just turning purple. I leaned down. "Everybody gets stage fright, Cory. Take a deep breath."

She shook her head. "I don't want to do this."

"Yeah, there are a lot of kids here. And they're all good musicians." My stomach heaved. Great idea. Cory and I would stall for time by both throwing up all over the place. *That is NOT an option,* I could hear Heather saying.

Cory squeaked.

"But you know what helps?" I continued. "Look around and imagine everyone wearing Muppet Babies underwear."

Cory choked and then started to giggle.

We sat up slowly and turned around. While Cory's skin returned to a normal color, I searched for Heather's face in the crowd.

Chapter **Sixteen**

A big woman in a long, flowery dress came through the double doors at the back of the auditorium and clapped her hands. Everyone turned to look at her. The hall quieted down.

"My, my," she gushed. "We are overwhelmed with excellence." She gazed around the auditorium. "Because of the success of our program this year, it is imperative that you sit in your assigned rows, in alphabetical order. You will perform in that order. After your age group has performed, you will be dismissed to the library, where you will await the judges' decisions. Is that clear?" She gave a little bow and disappeared out the door.

Everyone started talking and switching seats.

I looked at my watch. Three minutes to show time and still no sign of Heather. Cory poked me. She pointed to Nelson Able, sitting on the other side of her with his clarinet clutched to his chest.

"Nice underwear!" Cory mouthed to me and giggled. Cory was back to her old self again.

But I didn't have time for games now. I had to come up with a plan to stall.

A fire alarm. Scratch that. I didn't have any matches. What would I light on fire, anyway? My flute? Besides, the alarm was out in the hallway, right behind the check-in table—behind Iron Hair. Not a chance.

"Stall! Stall!" I kept saying to myself, but my mind was blank. I wished Caitlin were here. She could have done a gymnastics routine for everyone. The perfect warm-up act.

Then the judges filed onstage. Three men and four women, including the lady in the flowery dress. No Iron Hair, though, at least.

A friendly-looking man with large hands stepped forward to give the welcome speech. His voice boomed across the auditorium.

"You are all musicians," he began, but I didn't hear the rest of his speech. I was staring at the flag behind him. Stall, stall, stall . . .

Suddenly I heard polite applause. We were starting! I was going to have to do something. The crowd rustled behind me. A crowd about twenty times bigger than my French class. A fear monster grabbed me by the neck and filled my eyes with purple goo. I shook it off and checked the back doors. No Heather.

I jumped to my feet before I could talk myself out of it. "Wouldn't it be appropriate to say the Pledge of Allegiance first?" I called out.

The friendly man said something to the other judges. They looked at one another and nodded. "Very well, young lady," he said, "if you would like to lead us in it. Everyone, please rise." The judges stood and turned to the flag. Rows of students struggled to their feet behind me.

OK, I thought, trying to ignore my churning stomach. *Let's take this nice and slow.*

I'd never realized before how incredibly short the Pledge of Allegiance is. I looked back at the auditorium doors. Still no Heather.

Now what? The fear monsters were playing volleyball in my stomach, but I had an idea. I brought my flute up to my lips and started playing "The Star-Spangled Banner." The judges looked surprised but didn't try to stop me. So I just kept going. I played loudly, the notes coming out strong and clear.

One by one everyone joined in. Clarinets, trumpets, and baritone horns were all playing together. What a noise! When we finished, everyone cheered like it was the beginning of the World Series. It occurred to me that there were probably a lot of volleyball games going on in people's stomachs that morning.

It took about another three minutes for all of us to settle back down again. After that there was nothing more I could do. If only Heather would push open that auditorium door.

"Nelson Able," called out a judge. Nelson rose stiffly and made his way to the stage. Alphabetical order. Nelson, then Cory, then Heather. I looked at the empty seat next to me. Where *was* she?

Nelson finished his piece and stumbled off the stage. Cory was next. She gave me the thumbs-up sign as she scooted past me and walked up the steps. I barely heard her play before the next name was being called.

"Heather Bardlow."

The auditorium door banged open. Heather came bounding down the aisle with her flute in her hand and Suki bouncing in the baby carrier on her back. I almost didn't recognize her. Her frizzy hair was pulled back in a bun. She was wearing khaki pants, a white shirt, and a black vest. I couldn't see her socks, but I was betting that one was green and the other blue.

Suki smiled her biggest smile and patted Heather's bun with her chubby hand. For a minute, the hall buzzed in shock. I couldn't tell if it was from the surprise of seeing Suki, or from Heather's own electricity zinging through us all. Someone turned a laugh into a cough.

Heather paused by the foot of the stage to catch her breath. I held mine. Any minute Suki was going to start her "Mmee-mmee-MAAAA!" bellow, and the judges would throw them both out. But miraculously, Suki was quiet. She had discovered a new and amazing plaything—Heather's hair. As Heather walked up the stairs toward the judges, Suki was gleefully pulling strands of wispy blond hair straight up out of Heather's bun.

I clapped a hand over my mouth to stifle a groan. But Heather was totally unconcerned with her new hairdo. She nodded politely to the judges and took her place in the center of the stage. It seemed like everyone in the auditorium was holding their breath. You could have heard a pin drop.

"Heather, put her down!" I whispered.

"I can't. She'll cry," Heather mouthed back.

I slumped down in my seat. How was she going to play like that? Suddenly Iron Hair appeared from backstage, brandishing her clipboard. But the judge in the flowery dress waved her back.

"The Kuhlau, dear," the judge said gently to Heather.

Heather closed her eyes and brought her flute to her lips. She began to play, rising up like a swan—baby, backpack, and all. A soft stillness spread inside me. The fear monsters had disappeared, and Heather's music was taking their place, filling me up with cool, clear springwater. Now it was finally Heather's turn to wash everything clean. This was it.

Halfway through the piece, she opened her eyes. I thought she was looking at me, but then I realized that she wasn't seeing me at all. She was looking inward, maybe at the past, maybe at the future. Whatever it was gave her face a peacefulness that I had never seen before. The judges were all bobbing their heads in time to the music, as if nodding in agreement. Even Iron Hair was smiling.

Finally Heather finished, and it was my turn. I had a hard act to follow, but I didn't care. I was still floating on her music. I floated up to the stage, smiled happily at the judges, and hovered in front of the audience.

"The Beethoven, please," instructed the judge in the flowery dress. No sweat. I nodded to her politely, put my flute up to my lips, and flubbed the first three notes. All floating came to an abrupt halt. I jolted back to reality and looked out at a sea of horror-stricken faces. The other kids couldn't believe it either. The Beethoven was the easiest piece, and I had flubbed the first three notes!

I expected the fear monsters to devour me. But instead, the fourth and fifth notes came faltering out, more or less right. I kept going, and I completed the piece. I think I actually managed to make a little music near the end of it.

"I can't believe it's over," I said to Heather. We were sitting on the floor in the school library, picking up books that Suki had flung off the shelves.

"I can't believe she didn't scream," said Heather, taking a book out of Suki's mouth.

"How could she?" I replied. "The Kuhlau was amazing. You were really great, Heather."

"You were great too, Jenna."

I shrugged. "Well, the Beethoven was OK. 'The Star-Spangled Banner' was great!"

Heather choked back a laugh. "Yeah, so I hear! That was an *ex-treme* stall tactic, to say the least. I can't believe you did that." She looked down, then added quietly, "For me."

A messenger appeared in the library, ushering us

back to the auditorium. Suki let me carry her pig-gyback all the way to our seats. I swung her onto my lap as we sat down. "Now she lets me hold her," I said, rolling my eyes at Heather.

Iron Hair cleared her throat and tapped her clipboard with her pencil. "First, let me remind you that each and every one of you has proven him- or herself to be a capable and dedicated musician just by performing in this competition. Congratulations to all of you for striving to excel. Now, I am delighted to announce today's three winners. In third place, for the first time in the competition's history, we will honor a sixth grader: Heather Bardlow."

Heather jumped out of her seat and ran up the stairs to accept her award. The audience went wild. We were applauding the girl who played with the power of lightning and the grace of a swan, even with a squirming baby on her back. The newspaper photographer's camera flashed as Heather received her certificate for a year's worth of free flute lessons at Lakeville College. She was glowing like an angel.

I cheered like mad, clapping Suki's tiny hands between mine. It dawned on me that maybe going for great didn't mean you had to win something, like a flute competition or a gymnastics meet or the Crunchy-Crispos account. Maybe it just meant having the guts to keep trying. To keep wrestling with a crazed washing machine. To keep facing the music.

I thought about the Beethoven, and I found myself thinking, *Next time it will go better.* Yes, there would definitely be a next time.

Meet the Author

Carolee Brockmann

At age 13

Today

Carolee Brockmann studied both flute and piano throughout her school years, but singing has always been her major source of stage fright. Her jitters started with the backyard mini-operas that she staged in fifth grade with her sister. She continued to goof up solos all the way through college. Today she teaches middle school music and conducts children's choirs, helping students through their own nervous moments. She lives in New Jersey with her husband, son, daughter, and Portuguese water dog named Reggie.